Bystanders

by

Jonathan McKee

WP

WordServe Press

Centennial, Colorado

WordServe Press
A division of WordServe Literary
7500 E. Arapahoe Rd. Suite 285
Centennial, CO 80112
admin@wordserveliterary.com
303.471.6675

Cover Design: Aanivah Ahmed

Book Layout ©2013 BookDesignTemplates.com

Book Design: Greg Johnson

Ordering Information:

Quantity sales. Special discounts are available on quantity purchases by corporations, associations, and others. For details, contact the "Special Sales Department" at the address above.

Bystanders/Jonathan McKee, March 18, 1970

First Edition

ISBN 978-1-941555-38-5

PART I

"As men, we are all equal in the presence of death."

-Publilius Syrus

Author's Note: This book should be considered PG-13: language/violence

The Same

They grew up in the same suburb—Brett, Kari and Michael—
and crossed paths countless times.

Now they were in the same high school, even in some of the
same classes. But they never spoke a word to each other.

Until Tuesday.

Tuesday, 10:37 AM

In forty minutes it would begin.

He had traveled this road overlooking Cabrillo Park countless times, but never in this vehicle, and never with such focus. The park was just nine minutes from his school. He had timed it repeatedly.

The teenager carefully pulled the SUV to a stop in the shadows of a prune tree, shifting the vehicle in park, and letting the engine idle. He plugged in his phone and chose a song from his favorite playlist.

Rock Star Post Malone

He closed his eyes for a moment. These speakers had never been turned up so loud — his dad barely ever listened to the stereo. But the boy liked the noise. It helped numb the reality of what he was about to do. And he couldn't allow fear to get the best of him.

He found the music helped his mindset.

When my homies pull up on your block they make that thing go grrra-ta-ta-ta...

He opened his eyes.

His confidence was short-lived. The truth of what was about to happen was resting on his chest like a Buick. He pretended it wasn't there, trying to maintain his confidence. He tried to convince himself he was a sociopath — that he wouldn't feel what was about to take place. But he wasn't a sociopath. He felt nauseous.

He stepped from the SUV, head spinning, leaned over grabbing his stomach and lost what remained of his dinner from the night before. The boy hadn't bothered with breakfast. He couldn't eat. He reminded himself to try one of his mom's protein bars during the short drive to the school. He would need the strength, but he'd have to eat on the run.

Gotta keep on schedule.

The boy looked at his watch. 10:38. Two minutes ahead of schedule.

Regaining composure, he went to the rear of the Tahoe and opened the hatch, admiring the arsenal laid out before him. He reached for his AR-15 assault rifle, careful not to jar the scope. He had calibrated it perfectly, shooting watermelons in the desolate wilderness just outside of town.

Setting down the AR-15, he picked up the shotgun and checked the chamber. All loaded. It would take two hands to fire this beast, but that was okay, because he would have the Glock tucked away, and carry the assault rifle over his shoulder. Concealment wasn't important. There was no hiding what was about to be done.

He reached for the Glock, letting his hand slide around the grip smoothly and comfortably. He lifted the weapon up, sighting it on the trunk of the oak. The motion had become second nature to him with all the time he had spent shooting at squirrels and rabbits along the river.

He admired the fit of the weapon in his hand before tucking it into his belt. Then he fastened the homemade strap around his shoulder with its custom pockets for extra magazines and shotgun shells.

The boy glanced at his watch before unzipping the duffel bag to check its contents.

On schedule.

He inventoried the bag, its contents organized perfectly. Everything was accounted for. The recheck was unnecessary. The bag had been checked and rechecked a dozen times in the last eight hours. But everything must be perfect.

The teenager walked over to the barricade up on the hill overlooking the serene little park. His gaze swept across the children playing on the swings below.

Too young for school. Lucky.

They hadn't yet been forced to endure the inescapable taunts from peers, kids who might have even once called them friends. *Just wait. It will happen.*

Taking a deep breath, he hit the start switch on his timer.

PART II

. . . 28 hours prior

"Death is more universal than life; everyone dies but not everyone lives."

-A. Sachs

Michael, Monday 7:30 AM

Michael's pocket vibrated. It was Cordell.

Cordell: You up nigga?

His thumbs responded habitually.

Me: Yep. See you soon.

Cordell: Don't be late. Nana's riding my ass already.

Apparently, Michael had already missed a couple other texts while in the shower.

DB: Didn't finish my Algebra II.
Resident Evil marathon on HBO last night.

DB: Don't tell anyone I actually watched it.
They'll lose all respect for my movie palette.

Michael chuckled. Conversations with Deeby somehow always steered toward movies. He indulged his friend.

Me: Your secret is safe with me. If anyone asks,
I'll tell them you watched The Notebook.

Deeby replied in a wink.

DB: Only good Sparks book turned movie.
Wait… how do you know about that movie? That movie's old.

Me: Tish made me watch it with her.

DB: Ha. I wondered. You sister's hot! See ya in first.

Me: Deuces

Michael stumbled to the kitchen and poured a bowl of Cocoa Puffs.
Cocoa Puffs rule.

His mom came in and gave him a kiss as she grabbed her bank keys. She was a merchant teller at Northwest Bank. She counted all the big deposits from the local stores. Michael enjoyed hearing all her stories, especially the time she was robbed. Bank robberies are fascinating; and most bank robbers are incredibly stupid. Michael was intrigued with the escapades of stupid people.

Mom kissed him on the cheek. "You be good now." She raised her eyebrows, waiting for confirmation from his eyes.

"It's all good," Michael said, followed by another spoonful of Cocoa Puffs.

She playfully hit him in the arm with a quick right, keeping her left blocking her side and cracking a sly smile.

"Damn," Michael pouted, clutching his arm.

"Yeah right," she sighed. She dropped her fists, winked, and headed for the door.

Michael saw the clock click to 7:30 when mom closed the door behind her. Just like every morning, and then home at 6:40, an hour later on Fridays.

He put on some classic *Wiz Khalifa* and cranked up the sub.

We Dem Boys Wiz Khalifa

Michael always got ready to music.

> *Hol up, we dem boyz. Hol up, hol up, hol up, we makin' noise...*

Kari, Monday, 7:30 AM

The whistle of the air blowing through the little white Jeep was hypnotizing, even with the music blaring.

Kari shut her eyes and felt her hair dance in the wind as if it to the rhythm of the beat.

> *Closer*
> The Chainsmokers

She turned to the window and softly mouthed the lyrics.

We ain't ever getting older, we ain't ever getting older...

Her sister was playing an old playlist. Old, but good.

Kari opened her eyes and glanced around at Kristen and her friends. Kari felt way out of her league in this Jeep.

Kristen was Kari's older sister, gorgeous and a cheerleader, a toxic combination. Kari didn't care for cheerleaders, or her sister.

If only I looked like her.

Her sister Kristen was 5'8", a senior, and had a perfect body. Kari was only 5'3" with the body of a 7th grader. Her mom said she was still growing, but Kari was a sophomore and she figured, *if I was going to have boobs I'd have them by now!* So Kari tried to prepare herself mentally for going through life without them. Although she figured there were some benefits. Like in track — she ran the mile — she didn't have to deal with them pummeling her while she ran like Charlotte Bentley's did.

The Jeep made its routine right-hand turn into the Starbucks parking lot.

Eight minutes later, four girls emerged with cups in hand. Kari joined Megan in the back seat.

Apparently not all cheerleaders were bad. Megan Parks, who lived a block down from them, was actually really sweet. Megan usually sat in the back with Kari asking her about school and track. She actually talked to Kari in the school hallways, which didn't hurt Kari's popularity points since Megan was one of the prettiest cheerleaders in the school.

Then there was Taylor Withers sitting up front next to Kari's sister. Taylor was… well, she was a word Kari chose not to use. She always rode shotgun in Kristen's Jeep and painted on her makeup the entire way to school, complaining nonstop about her mom, guys, teachers, homework… you name it, she complained about it.

Regardless, the trips to school were tolerable. Plus, guys always saw Kari getting out of the car with three varsity cheerleaders. Granted, Kari was pretty sure they were looking at the cheerleaders, not her.

No one ever looks at me.

Brett, Monday, 7:30 AM

Brett placed the Red Bull on the counter.

The quick mart attendant scanned the drink robotically and glanced at his register. "Two thirty-six."

Brett pulled out a five and slid it across the counter, Abe Lincoln up.

While the man searched for quarters, Brett eyed a small rack of travel-sized meds displayed on the counter: Tylenol, Advil and SinuClear. Brett picked up the SinuClear bottle and began reading the label.

"Unbelievable," Brett sighed.

The man looked up at Brett, while cracking open a roll of quarters. "What?"

"Have you ever read the possible side effects of these medications?" Brett asked.

The man just looked at Brett.

"I mean, some of these side effects are worse than the original symptoms you're taking the meds for."

"Yeah," the man said, "but those are just *possible* side effects." He handed Brett his change.

"Exactly," Brett argued, sliding the change in his pocket. "They are *possible*. So anyone taking this drug must weigh the *possibility* of each of these symptoms… and listen to these." Brett read the label. "Headaches, dizziness, shortness of breath, heart palpitations, chronic diarrhea…"

Brett raised his eyebrows and looked at the attendant. "Chronic diarrhea? Really? What kind of tradeoff is that?"

The man waved his hand and sighed. "The pharmaceutical company just has to disclose that stuff. It isn't going to happen when you take the pills."

"That stuff *isn't* going to happen… or could *possibly* happen?" Brett asked.

The man looked confused.

Brett repeated the question, slower this time. "*Isn't*…or could *possibly*?"

"Isn't!" the attendant asserted.

"Then why is it on the label?"

The man pointed to the bottle. "Because if some jackweed takes these and gets the runs, then they can't sue and say, 'Hey, your meds made me soil myself on the way to work today!'"

Brett paused and looked at the man. "Soil yourself?"

"Yeah. You know... in your pants."

Brett leaned forward. "Have you ever 'soiled' yourself on the way to work?"

"No."

Brett cocked his head to the side, "Okay. Because you just sounded like you were speaking from first-hand experience there..."

"Well, I wasn't."

Brett continued without missing a beat. "...and if you were, I would think you'd agree with me that it would be prudent to avoid a medication claiming it could fix your sniffles at the cost of your boxer shorts."

The man grabbed the bottle out of Brett's hands. "Do you want to buy this or what?"

"Why would I want to buy something that will give me the runs and a heart attack?"

"Possibly!" the man roared, pointing to the label.

"Exactly," Brett said, snatching his Red Bull off the counter. "It is possible."

Brett held out his hands like he was weighing something in each hand. "*Hmmmmmm.* I could have the sniffles... or I could be nauseous, clutching my chest and soiling myself *with a clear nose!*"

Brett picked up his skateboard. "I'll take the sniffles, Amigo."

"I'm not a stupid Mexican," The attendant said, "I'm from Pakistan!"

Brett turned toward the door.

"*Racist.*"

Kari, Monday, 7:53 AM

The Jeep pulled into the parking lot a good ten minutes before the first bell. Plenty of time for Kristen and Taylor to catch up on the latest gossip and flirt with the entire football team.

The school was what most called a brat school. Mesa Rosa High School in Carmichael, California, near Sacramento. A school with mostly rich kids — *rich brats*.

But not all rich kids. There was an apartment complex on San Juan Avenue that fed into the school. Most of *those* kids walked or came on a bus, so the parking lot still reflected the incomes of the rich brats. Beamers, convertibles, new SUVs and even Kari's sister's little white Jeep.

As Kari stepped out of the Jeep she heard the screeching of wheels followed by the loud crunch of metal. Everyone ran toward the upper parking lot. Luke McCormick's gray Camaro had slammed into Courtney Veth's little red Civic. Kari loved that Civic…before it had a Camaro surgically implanted in its back end!

Courtney was standing next to her car screaming at Luke. Luke was inspecting her car scratching his head. Kari's sister and Taylor ran up to Luke and asked him if he was okay. Luke loved their attention. He fed off it.

Luke was the biggest tool at Mesa. He was like the bully in every teen movie. One would think when he saw any of those movies he would realize it. He'd stop and say, *Hey — I'm that guy. I'm a big douchebag!* But instead, he lived his life picking on everyone smaller than him — which was most of the school — and parading around in his stupid letterman jacket and wrestling shoes.

Kari was awestruck Kristen and Taylor didn't realize this. But apparently an unwritten code existed between athletes and cheerleaders — a code that swore loyalty, regardless of personality.

Megan and Kari stood watching Luke from a distance. They saw Taylor awkwardly lean into Luke and hug him, lifting her right leg like a flamingo.

Kari grimaced. "I think I just threw up in my mouth."
Megan laughed.
Kari said goodbye to Megan and headed to her first-period
class.
Her pocket vibrated. It was Niki.

NIK: Did you see Courtneys car?!!!

Kar Kar: Yeah. Yikes!!!

NIK: Gotta go. Huge test first period. FML ☹

Kar Kar: Hasta.

As she slid her phone back in her jeans she heard her name
being yelled across the quad. She was the only one named Kari
at the school. Two Carries, and one Kareigh, both pronounced
the same, but only one Kari. And since her name was pronounced like the *car* that you drive with *eee* on the end, Kari
knew someone was actually calling her.
She turned to see her friend Rebecca approaching.
"Did you see Luke's car?" Rebecca asked, tossing her stuffed
backpack over her shoulder.
"Yeah," Kari said. "Did you see what he did to Courtney's
Honda?"
"Oh. I know," Rebecca scrunched up her nose. "I loved that
car. Ugh! This backpack is so heavy. Was that Megan Parks?
She's so cool!" Rebecca had a gift with transitions.
"Yeah, she's the best. A rarity among cheerleaders," Kari said.
"I'm so glad she's going to Mexico with us."
"I know, right?"
Kari loved the trip. Last years proved to be one of the best
weeks she had ever experienced. Kari's sister Kristen always
thought Kari was crazy for saying that, but she never had gone.
She didn't understand why her sister would want to give up her
spring break to "roll in the dirt with dirty little kids in Mexico,"
Kristen always said.

The bell rang. Kari told Rebecca she'd see her later and headed for Algebra II.

I hate Algebra II.

Brett, Monday, 7:50 AM

Brett effortlessly shifted his weight from heel to toe, coasting down San Juan Avenue. He was used to the vibration on the bottom of his feet as his long board glided back and forth across the bike lane, against traffic.

Brett was enjoying the moment so much that he didn't notice the gray Camaro pass him and flip a U-turn 200 yards down the street. The Camaro caught Brett's eye when it started drifting in the bike lane about fifty yards in front of him.

The muscle car headed straight for him.

Brett's downhill speed made it hard to stop. After weighing the difference between the ditch to the left and the traffic to the right, Brett took his chances and tried to slow down with his foot. The momentum forced him off his board, and he lunged forward, taking 5 weighted strides, catching himself from falling, but losing his board into the street. The Camaro skidded to a stop right next to Brett just in time for him to see his board shoot under the back wheels of a utility trailer being pulled behind a huge Dodge that didn't even feel a bump. The board splintered before landing in several pieces in the median strip.

Catching his breath, Brett looked back toward the Camaro where Luke McCormick and three of his nameless friends were laughing hysterically. Luke regained his composure, rolled down the window and leaned across the front seat.

"I'm sorry," He offered dryly. "Was that yours?"

Brett fixed his eyes on Luke. He told himself Luke couldn't take anything away from him. Brett was already living twenty-four hours from now, and that kept him ticking.

If only you knew.

One of Luke's buddies leaned between the front two bucket seats. "We saw you on the side of the road and thought to ourselves, 'Self, we should pick up our friend Brett.' So we turned around to come give you a ride."

Luke interjected, "But it looks like you need some more practice with your long board!"

They all laughed, and the car peeled out down San Juan. Brett had hoped to show them that he wasn't afraid. He wanted them to know. But the fantasies he created in his mind never had happened. Yet.

Tomorrow.

Fifty feet down the road, the muscle car made another U-turn and headed back toward the school, slowing down as they passed Brett again.

Luke yelled out the window as they rolled by, "You better hurry up; you'll be late for school!" Luke gunned it, shifted, and the powerful Camaro's tires peeled out once again.

. . . tomorrow

Tuesday, 11:11 AM

He laid flat on the roof of the track house. He'd only been up here one time before when he was scouting locations a few months ago.

The view of the cafeteria was perfect.

The track house was a glorified shed full of track meet equipment located on the upper field of the school which happened to be less than 100 yards from the west side of the cafeteria.

The teen extended the legs of his rifle's bipod and looked through the scope. The main west doors going into the cafeteria were in clear view. Sixty yards, tops.

He glanced at the time on his watch. He never wore a watch, but he had bought one special for today. It read 11:13 a.m.

He cursed under his breath, disappointed for being behind schedule. One of the cafeteria workers was mopping the area where he had planned on setting his duffle bag along the north wall cubbies. It was the only spot where it wouldn't draw suspicion.

Every day a few hundred students would fill the cafeteria—he had counted. Most of them would come in from the west entrance and dump their backpacks and athletic bags in or near the cubbies. That area was daily littered with literally hundreds of bags.

When the cafeteria worker had finished mopping, the boy carefully double checked the time on his device and placed the bag in the perfect spot along the north wall. Guaranteed to kill hundreds and send the remnants dashing out the west doors. Few would use the east doors facing the parking lot and the ravine.

The delay had only cost him five minutes.

No worries. He'd built a little cushion into the schedule.

The teen took a breath and took in his surroundings. He placed earbuds in his ears, one at a time, then hit play on his phone.

> Suicide Machine
> Death

He breathed the music in.

Controlling their lives. Deciding when and how they will die...

He watched as students continued to fill the building. He had observed the building fill day after day. At 11:17 the building was usually filled to capacity. Sometimes over 400 students.

Looking through the scope he followed a blonde cheerleader walking with her friends toward the cafeteria doors. He practiced keeping the crosshairs on her as she moved... but then the scope started to shake.

The boy pulled his eye away from the scope. His hands were shaking. Something he had never experienced before.

He shook his hands and tried to psych himself up. The lyrics helped.

Prolong the pain. How long will it last? Suicide machine...

He looked at his watch and his heart started to beat even faster. It was 11:16 and 56 seconds, 57, 58, 59...

. . . the day prior

Luke, Monday, 7:53 AM

"Hey, that was third-gear scratch!" Luke said as he sped down San Juan toward the school.

"Yeah!" Tyler said. "You left half your tires back there!"

"And two pieces of a long board!" Blake said.

They all laughed as Luke hit 70 through the yellow light on Madison, blaring Drake, and almost catching air coming off the undulation.

```
Started from the Bottom
        Drake
```

The four had never experienced a hard day in their lives, but with music blaring they were pretty convinced they were living the hood life.

Started from the bottom now my whole team here…

Forty-five seconds later they pulled into the school's upper parking lot.

"Hey! There's Matt in his Yukon," Luke said, pulling up next to the shiny White SUV and rolling down his window. "Hey Matt! Wanna race?!"

Matt leaned over and flashed a big smile at Luke and rev'd up his engine. Luke kept looking directly at Matt as he floored it, squealing tires for the 4th time that morning.

Luke barely had time to touch the brakes when he heard Blake scream from behind and felt Tyler's grip on his leg. Luke only saw the little red Honda in front of him for half a second before he locked up and slid into it full force, moving it a good fifteen to twenty feet forward with the Camaro's bumper locked underneath.

Michael, Monday, 7:40 AM

Michael shoveled another bite of Cocoa Puffs into his mouth, music bumping, keeping beat with every chew. *Kanye's always got mad beats.*

> **Mercy**
> Kanye West, Big Sean, Pusha T & 2 Chainz

He caught a glimpse of his reflection in the microwave across the kitchen. His hair looked a little long. *I'll have to get Cordell to trim it again.* Cordell was real good at cutting hair. During the season he shaved all the team member's numbers on the backs of their heads. He said he's going to have his own barbershop someday. Michael and the other guys didn't tease him — about wanting to do hair — because Cordell was *huge!* No one messed with Cordell. Coincidentally, no one messed with Michael, either — a fringe benefit of being best friends with Cordell.

Michael stood up and threw his hands up:

All my broads is foreign. Money tall like Jordan

Tisha emerged from the bathroom in a cloud of perfume. "Hey 2 Chainz! Better not be late again or mom's going to kill you!"

"Good morning Tish," Michael said, flashing a fake smile.

Tisha squirted some lotion into her palm, snapped the cap closed with her chin and started lathering the lotion across her arms.

Michael knew she was right, but this was the game the two siblings played each morning. Tisha lectured, and Michael ignored her.

She stared at him with one of her hard looks for a minute. No one can mad dog like Tisha. She had mastered the evil eye. Michael stared right back and stuffed his face with Cocoa Puffs at the same time. A smile crept on her face and she finally broke her stare.

"I gotta go," she said, heading toward the door.

Lamborghini. Mercy. Swerve.

When Michael finally left his apartment complex on San Juan Avenue, he had to walk fast. If he was late one more time Mom would kill him.

The young man texted while he walked.

Me: You coming nga?

Cordell: Not yet

Me: I'm almost at ur house

Michael arrived at Cordell's house a few minutes later. They were late. He knew it because the sprinklers were off. Cordell's grandpa had the best-looking lawn on the block. His final watering cycle ended at 7:55. Michael knew that because the first bell rang at 8:03, and they learned early in the year that if the sprinklers were done already, then they were pushing it.

Cordell lived with his grandpa and grandma. His mom lived in L.A. and Cordell never talked much about his dad. His mom wasn't much better—dealing drugs out of South Central. Michael related. *Sounds like she should hook up with my dad.*

Once Nana got custody of Cordell, she raised him proper. Made him keep his grades up, and even brought him to church every Sunday.

Cordell opened the door before Michael got a chance to knock. He was talking to Nana as he walked out. "I know Nana, he's right here. We're going to be on time."

Nana followed him out the door. "Don't you talk back to me, boy. When I say you better get going, I only want to hear two words from you."

The almost 250-pound Cordell acted like a seventy-pound little kid around his grandma. "Yes ma'am," he answered cautiously.

"Morning, Nana," Michael said. Everyone respected Nana.

"Morning, Michael," she smiled slyly. "When you going to church with us?"

"I will soon, Nana. I promise."

A hard breeze blew past him as he uttered the words.

"I'll keep you to that," Nana said, pointing at him playfully. "Now you and Cordell use those legs that God gave you and get to school on time!"

"Yes, ma'am," they responded in unison.

Cordell and Michael hurried off toward the campus. His house was barely two minutes from the back entrance.

When they were out of range of his grandma's house, he finally spoke: "I don't know who rides my case more, Coach Reed or Nana."

Michael thought for a second. "Definitely Coach Reed. Especially yesterday," he said, picking up his pace to keep up with Cordell's gargantuan strides.

Cordell waved his head in disgust: "Coach was trippin.' He said I don't pass. I always pass." He hesitated for a second. "I shouldn't pass, but I do."

Michael didn't respond. There was no question Cordell was the best on the team. He proved that last season. Problem was: *he knew it.* Coach was right—Cordell *did* need to pass. Sometimes Cordell played one-on-five while the rest of the guys just watched. Sometimes he actually got away with it. He was that good.

As the two young men almost reached the school, Michael noticed Cordell stop and stare over his shoulder. When Michael turned around he saw what Cordell was looking at: Nicole and Sierra were walking across the back parking lot. Cordell knew Michael liked Sierra Blake. Michael didn't know Sierra well, but he had talked to her a few times in the hallway or after school. Once he was lucky enough to walk home next to her. It seemed like they hit it off. Michael got her number anyway, and they had texted since.

Michael watched her as she gently tucked a strand of her hair behind her ear. Cordell finally broke the silence, talking into his hands like an intercom. "Michael. Earth to Michael!"

Michael shook his head. "Huh?"

Cordell wasn't paying attention. His eyes were fixed on the school parking lot.

"What?" Cordell gasped, putting his hand to his mouth in disbelief. "Is that Courtney's Civic?"

Michael pried his eyes off of Sierra. A crowd of people were gathered in the upper parking lot looking at a wreck that looked like Luke McCormick's Camaro and Courtney Veth's Civic. Michael loved that Civic. It had tinted windows, ground effects and a bumpin' stereo.

"That is," Michael finally responded. "… and Luke's Camaro!"

The two boys strode over there, not looking too curious. Unspoken rule number one on campus: don't look excited for anything. Just play it cool no matter what comes at you. It's part of the image. Two of Michael's friends were hanging by the flagpole gawking at the wreck. Deeby Pearage saw them coming and wandered over holding out hammered fists in a greeting.

Cordell greeted them with a pound of the fist. Their friend Jared filled them in. "Can you believe this? Luke peeled out trying to be all fast and furious, and WHAM! He smacked into the back of Courtney!"

"*Fast Five*," Deeby interjected. "By far the best one."

They all ignored him. Deeby was a walking movie encyclopedia. You couldn't enter a conversation with him without him bringing up some movie reference.

A crowd gathered around the wreck, gawkers, sipping their Starbucks. Michael chuckled.

What's with white girls and Starbucks?

Tension grew even more unsettled by Courtney's car. Michael had never seen her so mad. Her face was as red as her Honda. She was yelling at Luke who was trying to defend himself, with no luck. It was kinda funny watching someone yell at Luke. If it were a guy doing the yelling, Luke would have probably dropped him by now. But even Luke seemed to know not to hit a girl, even one yelling in his face.

Luke wasn't too bright. A junior. A jock. A tool. Michael had him in two classes: Algebra II and P.E. One step behind everyone else mentally, so he had to beat up everyone to try to earn a few points.

No one messed with him. No one could, except Cordell. But the two of them never had a reason to go at it. If they did, it would be an incredible fight. Luke went to State as a wrestler the last two years. He let everyone know it, too—wore his wrestling shoes every day. But Michael would put his money on Cordell.

Cordell grew up in the hood before he moved in with his grandma. Got beat up almost every day by his dad. When you get beat up by an adult every day, high school kids just aren't that much of a threat.

Once Michael saw Cordell get into a fight with a guy at Oakview High after a basketball game. This fool tried to disrespect him in front of a bunch of people. Cordell just set down his bag, walked right up to the guy and got in his face.

The trash-talker surprised us all and hit Cordell in the forehead, just above the right eye in the eyebrow. No one was sure if he was aiming for his eye or what, but the punch landed on his forehead. The next few moments were clear in Michael's mind; it's like time froze. Cordell just stood there staring at the guy.

The guy started to say something, but Cordell grabbed him, literally lifting him up over his head, and threw him through a window in the portables by the pool. Michael grabbed Cordell's bag and ran ahead. Cordell just walked, blood rolling down from his right eyebrow.

Michael smirked, thinking about it.

Cordell would probably deliver the one fight that Luke might not just walk away from.

Mr. Sanders, the vice principal, was out in the parking lot by Luke's accident already, and so was Large Marge—the school officer who tried to bust people sneaking on or off campus. She attained the name Large Marge because she made Courtney's Civic look like a Hot Wheel.

Michael chuckled when he saw Large Marge waddling about. She was waving her finger at Luke and pointing to the car, no doubt interfering in something she didn't know anything about, like teachers do.

The adults at Mesa Verde have issues.

Michael paused for a moment and amended his thought.

Except for Mrs. Allison.

Mrs. Allison, Monday, 7:40 AM

"Damn!"

Nancy Allison noticed the car seat in the back of her minivan. Biting her lip, she looked at her watch. She didn't have time to switch the car seat to Derek's Sentra. It was his day to take Gage to daycare.

Why didn't we just buy two car seats?

She pulled the car seat from the back seat of the minivan and quickly set it on the hood of Derek's car. A handful of suicidal Cheerios cascaded to the garage floor, nestling themselves in one of many large cracks in the cement.

She considered strapping it in the backseat for him, but she didn't have time.

I'll probably hear about this later.

As she pulled up to the first stop sign, she plugged her phone into the USB port. Her playlist resumed from yesterday, featuring another one-hit wonder she loved from yesteryear.

How Bizarre
OMC

Nancy would describe her marriage of five years as "happy" and "fulfilling." That wasn't too far from the truth. She truly felt that way at times. It's just that Derek always wanted things done a certain way. Nothing mean or abusive. Just frustratingly obsessive.

Don't put the leftovers in a Cool Whip container without labeling them or I won't eat it.

Leave your phone on so I can get a hold of you.

Don't put my sunglasses in the drawer when I leave them on my dresser, because then I can't find them.

Nancy clenched her teeth thinking about that one. "Then don't leave your freaking sunglasses on the dining room table every day!" she thought out loud, cornering her Honda Odyssey a little too fast for the residential street.

She tapped her hands to the beat on the steering wheel:

How bizarre. Ooh baby, ooh baby. It's making me crazy...

Nancy met Derek at age twenty-four in her "Film as Communication" class at California State University in Sacramento, or "Sac State," as the locals call it. Derek took the class because it was in his major. Nancy signed up for the class because she loved film and simply needed the three units.

Nancy took notice of Derek when he spoke out against Peter Bogdanovich's 1971 classic, *The Last Picture Show*. Nancy remembers the sighs from around the classroom. She had kept quiet, but secretly agreed with Derek.

Two days after the class she saw Derek sitting by himself in the Student Union highlighting passages from what looked like a philosophy textbook.

"Planning on talking trash about *Citizen Kane* tomorrow?" Nancy jested.

The rest was history.

The first three years of marriage were the hardest for them: broke, overworked, and both a little too immature and stubborn to back down in an argument. But by year four it seemed as though both of them learned to choose their battles. The pendulum swung in year five. They found themselves repressing their feelings and communicating less, until finally the unavoidable day when one of them exploded in an argument and lashed out with mean words that were quickly regretted.

Last night, for example, after they got back from one of his work parties downtown.

The phone vibrated from its place in the cup holder, rattling loose change. Nancy fetched the phone with her right hand, pressed her thumb on the reader, unlocking it without even taking her eyes off the road. Lifting the phone to her field of view she read the text.

D: Love you kiddo!

She hit one button and dropped the phone back in the cup holder.

Right now, her mind was on the *Of Mice and Men* test she was going to be giving 1st, 4th and 5th period. She would deal with Derek later.

Time would heal everything.

It always had.

How bizarre!

Nancy navigated her Odyssey into the school parking lot, quickly finding an open spot in the shade of the faculty parking lot. She peeked into the mirror on the visor, checking her lipstick, then poked the button to open the automatic sliding doors.

She grabbed her bag from the back seat and hit the button on her remote to close the door—and she stood there and watched it close. Derek always teased her for doing this habit. "What? Do you think it's going to open back up again?" he'd say. Nancy now wanted to watch it close even more, maybe just to spite his jeering.

Derek wasn't such a bad guy. He was actually very charming. But outside of those charming moments, he had a system for everything. Some might call him meticulous. Others would call it tiresome.

But Nancy was a big girl and never one to let someone walk over her. Five years as an MP taught her that. She still wrestled with some of the vivid memories from her Army days with the 82nd Airborne Division on the outskirts of Fallujah. Derek's antics were easily manageable in comparison… sometimes even cute.

Besides, he was ruggedly handsome, and he dressed impeccably.

As the door closed, she began walking toward the sidewalk. Her 5'6", thin frame had softened a little since the birth of Gage, but her beauty was undeniable. She had no idea how many heads turned in a crowd to watch the eye-catching brunette walk by each day.

A male voice greeted her from behind, a voice she recognized all too well. "Good morning, Nancy."

Nancy turned with a smile. "Good morning, Dan."

Dan Travers was the Junior Honors History teacher. He was six feet tall, at least 200-pounds—none of it fat, with dark eyes, wavy brown hair and a chiseled jawline. Nancy was a married woman, and she never wanted to look around at anyone else. She loved Derek, and despite their differences, they *were* married. But Nancy wasn't blind. Dan was something straight out of a daytime soap, with a chin like Ryan Reynolds and a sandy voice like Mark Ruffalo. He actually reminded her of a guy she dated back when she was in the Army.

"I see you drove the family wagon again today," Dan said, keeping stride with Nancy, and nodding back toward the Odyssey.

"Yes," Nancy replied. "The Porsche is in the shop and the Hummer just doesn't get the gas mileage that the ol' minivan does."

Dan laughed, displaying a smile pristine enough for a toothpaste commercial.

Nancy smiled, not quite sure if it was a genuine response or a courtesy smile. She was torn. She definitely enjoyed her little conversations and jesting with Dan, but she often sensed there was something under the surface of their joking. That thought scared her. She felt guilty even noticing that Dan made her feel warm and relaxed.

Another voice called from across the parking lot as Nancy and Dan stepped onto the sidewalk toward campus.

"Nancy. Hold on for a minute."

This voice was far from warm and relaxing. Nancy did all she could do to not shudder when she heard the scratchy beckoning. The voice belonged to Mrs. Hippo. Yes, that was really her name, and she had a girth to match. She was one of the vice principals and seemed to actually enjoy making others suffer. She was unorganized and a micromanager, a lousy combination.

"Nancy," Mrs. Hippo howled from across the parking lot. "I need to talk with you about the STAR testing scores." Nancy couldn't figure out if Mrs. Hippo was a closet chain smoker or if she was just desperately trying to impersonate one of Marge Simpson's sisters.

Nancy turned to Dan. "I guess this is my cue."

"Enjoy!" Dan offered, tucking his tail and doubling his pace.

Part of Nancy was relieved to have an excuse to end the conversation with Dan. If only for any other reason.

Nancy watched as the hefty vice principal waddled toward her. Her subconscious recalled a commercial from her childhood, an ad for a children's board game. Voices singing, *"Hungry Hungry Hippos…"* Nancy covered her mouth, doing all she could to not snicker.

Her thoughts were interrupted by a deafening crash from the upper parking lot, not 100 yards away. Nancy and Mrs. Hippo both turned to see a gray Camaro grafted into the back of a little red Honda Civic, both rolling forward to a stop.

Hippo exhaled loudly. "What now?!" And marched off toward the accident.

Nancy stood on the sidewalk for a second, watching from a distance. A young girl got out of the Civic and began yelling at a boy she recognized as Luke McCormick. No one seemed hurt.

Mrs. Hippo continued waddling toward the cars with purpose.

Nancy shook her head.

Hippo always wanting to be the cop.

Investigator John Grove, Monday, 8 AM

Investigator John Grove of the Sacramento County Sheriff's Department made his way down the flickering fluorescent hallway that led to his office. He managed a smile and gave a nod as he passed Ann from the DA's office but didn't say anything—his mind was elsewhere.

His investigation of a recent outbreak of gang activity in Citrus Heights had led him to a disturbing discovery of drug dealings and weapons sales emerging from a small neighborhood called Cranhaven.

Cranhaven was merely a horseshoe shaped street with a bunch of cul-de-sacs and bisecting streets branching off it. But students living in the area had become territorial over the years and actually referred to the area as if it were a city. The predominant gang activity in the area stemmed from a group that called itself CHC, the "Cran Haven Crips." CHC started in the late 80s, with a few punks stealing cigarettes and starting small skirmishes in the streets. But this quickly escalated, especially with the growth of gangster rap in the early 90s.

John, now in his forties, remembered the music he listened to in his first years of college. It was then, in 1987, that the music industry underwent a change. A young drug dealer out of Compton named Eric Wright joined forces with a young artist named Dr. Dre. The world awoke to a new era when their first creation hit the record stores: *N.W.A. and the Posse*, N.W.A being an acronym for *Niggaz With Attitude*. Eric, who went by the name "Easy E," became one of the boldest and loudest voices for young black men. A voice that made many black people proud but probably would have made Dr. King shudder.

Despite what some might say, *N.W.A. and the Posse* was really the dawn of the gangster rap era.

Cops remember these days well, especially 1989 when the album *Straight Outta Compton* was released. Stores never sold so many Raiders jackets, parkas, and beanies. When John would go home from school to visit his brother, he and all his little friends were wearing Raiders apparel, walking and talking like gangsters. After all, that's what Easy E, Ice Cube, and Dr. Dre wore. *And now kids know Ice Cube for his acting.*

John threw his jacket on the back of his chair and glanced at the sticky notes on his phone as he sat down. He leafed through a pile of folders on his desk. What had started with a phone call from an older lady living in Cranhaven (even the police had adapted that label) had exploded into an enormous investigation now involving narcotics and homicide.

John's fingers stopped on a manila envelope near the top of his pile.

He sipped his coffee and wiggled the envelope from the pile, careful not to spill coffee on his shirt. John was not only six-foot-three and built like a linebacker, he was the best-dressed guy in his squad. His wife Manda always pressed his shirts and affirmed he looked like Denzel on Steroids.

The envelope bore the words *Brett Colton* written in red Sharpie. John worked open the envelope with one hand and removed a folder from Glenn Hicks, another investigator in his office. As John leafed through the folder, he quickly realized that Hicks had merely passed the buck with this one, a phenomenon not too unfamiliar in the department. Every investigator has a workload far exceeding the necessary time to complete it, so they had each learned early on to delegate or "pass the buck" when any opportunity to do so arrived.

John saw why the pass was allowed—this sophomore at Mesa Rosa High School had been accused of issuing a death threat back in January. Upon investigating the student, they found him interacting with a group of probable drug dealers in Cranhaven.

John fingered through the stack, stopping on the first page of a report where a four-by-three picture of a boy was attached with a paper clip. He was sitting on the grass with a Golden Retriever. Probably fifteen or sixteen, he was small and pale with sandy blonde hair and wearing loose black clothing. His eyes were small and dark with a determined look in them.

John always noticed eyes.

He had toyed with art in college and often sketched faces. The shapes of eyes always fascinated him. Manda's eyes, for example, were large and round with dark lashes. John had sketched her eyes many times. He knew them by heart. He could get lost in those eyes.

The boy in the picture held his head low as if he were shy . . . but his eyes were on full alert, as if they were catching every movement in the yard around him. His pupils were dilated, almost blending in with the dark brown color surrounding them—the whites of his eyes, barely visible. The folds on his eyelids bowed under the force of his clenched brow, as if it was holding an enormous weight.

John's own eyes wandered off the picture down to one of Investigator Hick's reports. *Now this was funny.* Investigator Hicks stopped to see this Brett Colton at his house. On the way to the house, Hicks almost ran a teenager over with his car as "a juvenile wearing a black T-shirt," the report read, "darted in front of him on his skateboard."

Hicks probably was looking at his GPS, the careless idiot.

The report continued, "Upon knocking on the door, the mother verified that her son just left . . . *wearing a black T-shirt.*"

John chuckled. *You almost killed the kid you were supposed to question.* This is where it became funny. Hicks asked the mother for a picture. She obliged.

According to the report, Hicks popped in his car and turned toward the direction he saw Brett heading. He actually saw him skateboarding in the Walmart shopping center—toward Cranhaven. So Hicks clicked into surveillance mode, followed him and eventually observed the young teen go to the house of one Jason Dewmore.

Dewmore.

John set his coffee down and leaned forward in his chair. He knew the name well.

He kept reading. Apparently, Hicks had recognized the house as it was under investigation by Narcotics and Robbery /Homicide. Both weapons and drugs, had been traced back to that house. Hicks saw Brett Colton hand someone at the house an envelope.

Drugs?

John leaned back in his chair and kicked his feet up on his bottom drawer.

Small world, John thought. This house was the same one that John's attention had been focused on for the last few weeks. In fact, John's entire investigation had led him to that house. He and his boys had big plans for that address tomorrow morning.

John kept reading. Apparently, this kid Brett got on his board and headed out of Cranhaven through another street. Hicks tried to follow but got stuck waiting for a lady trying to get her kids outta the street. Hicks honked at the lady who then "verbally attacked" him and pounded on his hood. Hicks eventually arrested her for 148 p.c (interfering with a police officer). John glanced at the arrest report and booking picture for Gina Jackson. He leaned back in his chair laughing. John knew the neighborhood well and could picture the situation clearly. Hicks probably tried to get an attitude with Jackson for getting in the way. John just shook his head smiling. *Hicks, you stupid white boy. Never get an attitude with a black woman!*

John figured that by the time Hicks had put all this information in a report—never confirming the contents of the envelope—he knew he had nothing. Besides, Brett Colton was small potatoes compared to Dewmore. *The file must have set on his desk for a couple of months before he thought of passing it to me,* John concluded.

John stared at the photo once again. The boy's pale arm was resting on the dog, his hand scratching the dog's head. The dog was completely content, but the boy seemed . . . removed, absent. Physically present, but mentally somewhere else.

John blinked twice and shut the folder. *Another case for my "to do" pile.* John stuffed the folder in the envelope and threw it on his pile. He would follow up on it. That's the kind of cop John was. But it would have to wait. He made a mental note to check into it after tomorrow morning's bust.

He snorted as he saw the next day's date on his desk calendar. April 20. Kind of ironic busting a known drug dealer on that date.

Instagram that mug shot, Dewmore, holding that date in your hands. It'll go viral.

His phone chimed from the desk. John grabbed it.

Manda: Hey sexy! ♡♡

John chuckled and typed with both thumbs.

JG: You are the light of my day!

John slid three paperclips off his desk into his drawer.
Chime.
Manda: ☺

John smiled, tucked the phone in his pocket, and grabbed his jacket.

Kari, Monday, 8:07 AM

When Kari arrived at Algebra II, a freshman darted through the doorway in front of her, eager to get to his seat.

Three freshmen were in this class, making the rest of the roster feel dumb, but not as dumb as Kenny Baker felt. Kenny was the guy with the long curly hair who sat in front of Kari. He was a junior and was taking this for the second time. If he loved Algebra II one tenth as much as he loved his drum set, then he would probably pass.

Kari took her seat and fetched her completed homework. It made her feel accomplished, at least for the next few minutes before Mr. Colfax would confuse her with today's lesson.

I loathe this class.

Misty Tucker leaned over and whispered, "I guess Brett isn't going to be joining us today."

Kari looked, and Brett's chair was empty. No one liked Brett. He wore janky clothes, even painted his nails sometimes. The guy literally had no friends. He sat in front of Misty, and she was always glad when he was gone.

Kari offered her sarcastic condolences: "I'm sorry. I know you'll miss him."

Misty rolled her eyes.

Mr. Colfax started class the same as every morning, collecting homework.

After passing the homework forward, he dropped a bomb. "Pop quiz."

Kenny Baker turned around, chewing his gum louder than most human beings—louder than most horses—could chew. "Don't you just live for first-period math?"

Kari feigned her best fake smile. "Kill me now!"

Michael, Monday, 8:05 AM

Michael made pretty good time because he actually got to Algebra II a couple minutes early—it was only half full.

He grabbed his seat in the back. Mr. Colfax had a seating chart. Michael lucked out at the beginning of the year and got a back-row seat. He didn't feel like pulling his homework out, so he just sat there and watched people come inside.

Michael liked watching people—you learn a lot. You can tell which girls are insecure, worrying about what guys think about them. Little clues like seeing them cast quick glances around to see if anyone is watching. Or you see them pull out mirrors, checking their make-up again and again, or checking their hair multiple times in a five-minute timespan.

Guys aren't much better. You can see them sucking in their guts as they walk in the classroom, adding a little bounce to their swag. Then you see them trying to talk with the girls around them. Some of them have no game. It's embarrassing to watch sometimes.

Michael watched this freshman named Brandon King scurry in and take his seat. He was one of the smart kids in the class, and he never seemed too worried about what others thought. He wasted no time pulling out his homework and immediately organizing it.

Then Michael noticed this girl Kari Ridge come in, Starbucks in hand. She was a rich little church girl. She was smart. She just didn't have a clue what life was like beyond her white picket fence and brick mailbox.

Michael couldn't help but notice she wasn't bad looking; in fact, she probably could be hot someday. She just seemed a little too… *young?*

She took her seat right away and started talking with a girl next to her named Misty. Michael didn't catch what they were talking about at first but then he realized they were laughing about a guy in their class named Brett.

Michael looked over to Brett's seat. He wasn't there, and Michael wasn't exactly sad about that. This kid Brett was one of the most interesting ones to watch. Every day when Brett walked in the classroom, he never looked at anyone—at least until he sat down. He just went straight to his seat and dropped back into an immediate slouch. His head always stayed real low, with his chin in his chest. Michael didn't catch it at first, but Brett watched people, too. He never moved his head, but his eyes— *his creepy small eyes*—were always looking to the left and the right, watching people's every move.

Michael can't necessarily blame him. Brett might have just been watching out for Tyler, Blake or some of the other guys in this class who messed with him daily. Michael wondered if Brett had ever gone through just one day in his high school existence without Blake or one of the other guys knocking his books off his desk.

Michael didn't know how it actually began. Brett was not a bad guy, or, at least, he used to not be so pathetic. Michael's friend Nick actually hung out with Brett in middle school. They both were really into video games. Other than Madden, Michael wasn't into games. But apparently Nick and Brett would play Xbox Live together and battle each other all the time.

But Brett didn't hang out with anyone now. Michael always saw him alone. Seems like he almost enjoyed it that way.

And students messed with Brett more than just in this class—especially in gym class. A few weeks ago, Luke McCormick and Tyler Copeland slapped the back of his neck real hard as they walked by in the locker room. It was real cold out. Must've hurt like hell.

But when Brett was slapped he didn't even flinch; he just looked up at them like a tiger would look at you from inside his cage, waiting for someone to accidentally leave the latch open. Creeped Michael out.

Michael's eyes wandered over to the other side of the room where Misty and Church Girl were laughing and talking about Brett.

Michael shook his head.

Deeby came meandering in about a minute before the bell rang and plopped down behind his desk immediately to Michael's left. "Alrighty then."

Another movie quote, Michael presumed, since Deeby's mind was a database of movie knowledge. That's actually what provoked his nickname: DB. Short for IMDB, The Internet Movie DataBase. Deeby was the type who watched a movie, then watched the Blu-ray special features, then watched the movie again listening to the audio commentary. It took this boy like nine hours to watch just one of the *Hobbit* films.

But Deeby was hilarious in this class—amazing comic relief. He only spoke in movie quotes. Michael didn't recognize half of what he said.

It was Jake's fault. On the second day of class Jake had made a $100 bet with Deeby that he couldn't make it through the entire quarter only saying movie quotes in this class. Jake was stupid for making the bet. Deeby speaks almost exclusively "movie" anyways. But now it was official. Even if Mr. Colfax asked him a question, Deeby had to speak in movie quotes. But Deeby didn't care.

Mr. Colfax strutted in as the bell was ringing and didn't waste any time. "Get out your homework and pass it forward."

Michael pulled out his three pages of homework and passed it forward. Deeby pulled out half a page and did the same.

Slouching back in his chair he turned to Michael. "You're so wise. You're like a miniature Buddha covered in hair."

Michael snickered, finally recognizing one. But his smile didn't last long.

"Pop quiz." Colfax announced.

Everyone groaned, as if on cue.

Mrs. Allison, Monday, 8:10 AM

Nancy put on her best poker face for her freshman in first period Honors English. Her mind was at home replaying her exchange of words with Derek the night before.

But *Of Mice and Men* wouldn't wait.

"Get out your pens everyone. It's that time." She picked up a stack of freshly printed tests off her desk.

Groans resounded throughout the classroom. Funny. No matter how much the students were prepared, no one enjoyed exam day.

She handed out a stack of exams to the first person in each row. "All of the questions are essay. Don't worry. No surprises. It's what we discussed in class. But this is your chance to put your thoughts on paper."

More groans.

"Come on people," Nancy quickly responded. "This is easy stuff. Plus, we're getting it over with early in the week. Maybe we'll even watch a movie on Friday since it's the last day before break."

The class didn't seem appeased. No matter.

"You're all gonna do great!" she offered as a final indulgence. "Now get to work."

Pacing the front of the room, Nancy watched as the students read through the three essay questions. One by one around the room, pens began to fill the blank pages.

Returning to her desk, Nancy reached for her purse. She kept her phone out of sight behind the desk.

3 text messages have arrived. Select "Go to"

Derek, she thought to herself.

Yep.

D: Just dropped Gage off at daycare. I'm so sorry about last night baby. i was dumb. I love you so much.

D: I'm at a break at work. Call me if you get a chance.

D: Are you there?

Nancy stared at the buttons on her phone for a moment. She looked around the room. Most the students were engrossed in their essays. Tiffani, a petite little girl who looked not a day older than twelve, was staring at the ceiling and tapping her pen between her teeth. Two aisles over, Craig was gripping his hair with both hands as if massaging his scalp would help him write.

Sheesh. It's not that bad, Craig.

It was strange having the classroom so silent. The sound of pens frantically gliding across the paper was barely audible above the whistle of air from solitary vent in the ceiling. Distant voices were heard in the hallway.

The sound of wheels outside the classroom grew louder. Clint, the janitor, walked past pushing his maintenance cart. His hair was dark, greying at the sides, but trimmed high and tight. His stained shirt hung from his torso as if dressed on a scarecrow. Same shirt every day, it seemed, with rolled up sleeves, exposing the man's scaly tatted arms.

He glanced in the classroom and connected eyes with Nancy, nodding politely and quickly returning his gaze to the hallway in front of him.

Nancy shuddered. *The guy seriously creeped her out.*

As he rolled out of sight, she returned her attention to her phone. She typed with her thumbs.

Nancy Pants: In class. Can't talk now.

She hesitated for a second.

Nancy Pants: Love you too. ♡

Michael, Monday, 11:10 AM

When lunch arrived, students filled the hallways lethargically, relieved to be out of class, but markedly conscious that it was still only Monday.

Michael found Cordell and the team in the student center.

The student center was a pretty good-sized room… if you could even call it a room. It was really just a place where the hallway was wide in this zig-zag area upstairs in the Drake building.

Years ago, Tisha's senior class had decided that their school didn't have a cool place to hang out at lunch or after school. The campus lacked a large quad area outside like most schools in California. Aside from the gym, the cafeteria and two small administration buildings, the campus mainly consisted of the Drake building which was a big two-story building containing all of the major classrooms. So this group of seniors did a fundraiser, carpeting this area in the Drake building. They collected half a dozen old couches, added a few tables, chairs, and a sound system and labeled it *The Student Center*.

Everyone liked it because it was a cool place to just hang and there was always music playing. MJ was playing at the moment. Old school hit.

P.Y.T.
Michael Jackson

That could only mean one thing. Michael glanced over to the corner of the room where the sound system was controlled.

Yep. Ashley.

Michael didn't know much about this girl, but she had some amazing playlists. New stuff, old classics… all good. Everyone always liked it when Ashley was DJ'n.

Michael continued scanning the room. Plenty of cheerleaders. Football players flocked to the cheerleaders like fat kids to a taco.

But Michael wasn't interested in cheerleaders today. He was looking for someone else.

Cordell must have noticed Michael's lack of interest in the immediate surroundings. "What you thinkin' bout?" He asked. "You're all quiet."

"Nothin." Michael didn't look at Cordell at first. But then a sly grin gave him away and he peeked at Cordell.

"Oh," Cordell grinned. "I see. I ain't seen her, neither." He knew Michael too well.

"Saw Nicole over by the snack bar a while back," Michael added. "Sierra wasn't with her either."

The two boys sat for a moment enjoying MJ:

I Want To Love You, P.Y.T. Pretty Young Thing...

"Let's dip out and go over to the cafeteria," Cordell finally offered. It was nice of him to sympathize with Michael. "Maybe she's in there and we missed her."

The two of them walked down the hallway toward the stairs, passing a few freshman classrooms still in session at the end of the hall. They had B Lunch. B Lunch is the worst.

It sucks to suck!

They slowly strutted over to the cafeteria.

Most of the students had filtered into their routine spots by now.

A bunch of the smart kids filled a table, laughing about something. Michael knew they were smart because he was in their Honors English class every year. Michael was always good in English, writing papers and interpreting poetry. He also did really well in vocabulary. He liked words. He just didn't necessarily want to use them in front of his friends.

Being in Honors English made his mom proud. She had high hopes that Michael would become a writer someday. Michael had convinced her now to at least say "sports writer."

Michael had to give credit to Mrs. Allison — his freshman Honors English teacher. Not only was she hot, she somehow made the study of literature fun. Michael never liked English until Mrs. Allison. She was amazing. Best teacher he ever had. He wished he could say the same about his Honors History teacher, Mr. Shaw, but this guy was literally the worst teacher ever. Michael wasn't alone in his opinion. Girls thought this guy was straight up creepy, as in, Clint the janitor creepy. On a scale of zero to ten, ten being creepy, Mr. Shaw was a twelve.

The only thing Michael liked about that history class was debating. Students got to act out debates, taking sides on the issues we were studying. Michael was always good at debating. He analyzed what people said and dissected it piece by piece. This was a good thing in intellectual discussions — a bad habit in his personal life. People don't like their words being used against them. Like his old teacher Mr. Shaw for instance. Michael lasted barely one quarter in that class before talking his mom into letting him take normal history. She finally caved and let him switch.

Mr. Shaw probably went out and partied the night he got the note Michael was switching. *No worries,* Michael thought. He'll think twice before ever trying to tell Custer's story *his way* again.

Everyone in the cafeteria was in their own little group today. Everyone but Brett.

Brett was sitting by himself again. Probably because Luke was up at the student center — Brett kept his distance from Luke.

Cordell was talking with some junior girls sitting at a table next to them, so Michael pretended to be in the conversation, but he was watching Brett. Brett was just sitting there in one of the overstuffed chairs in the lounge area by the lobby. He had his backpack and a notebook on his lap and was just staring across the room. Something wasn't right. Michael didn't know what, but Brett wasn't right in the head.

Lunch was 45 minutes. Before long, it was 11:50-something, which meant the bell would ring soon.

Michael never could remember the exact times. He didn't know who originally figured out the school times, but they didn't make sense. Why start school at 8:08? Why not 8? Why not 8:30? No... 8:08. And what time is lunch? 11:08 or something like that. Why not 11:30? How about noon?

A white guy must have planned this schedule!

The bell rang, and the boys headed to P.E. Michael and Cordell had weights together. Michael loved it. This was the first year he lifted so he was able to really increase his max. He started benching 120 at the beginning of the year. He tried not to advertise that, especially when the football players who had been in weights all four years were benching 200 or 300 plus. But Michael was excited because he weighed 140 and now his bench was up to 165. Pretty good for a sophomore. He figured he'd break 200 next year.

Luke McCormick actually showed up for P.E. class, even though he had missed Algebra II. Probably getting his car towed. Usually he was loud, joking with Tyler and some of the other fellas. But today he was quiet . . . and everyone knew why. Everyone was staying clear of him. Michael figured, *let the guy suffer in peace.*

This class was the easiest class of the day. Do a few exercises and then hang out with the boys. Maybe even lift a few weights. Since Nick, Deeby and Cordell were all in this class with Michael, he always had a good time.

Fifteen minutes later, having finished roll call and stretching, they resumed running laps around the lower field. Coach always had them running.

"The average NBA player runs three to five miles in a game!" he would always tell them.

Coach was wrong. Michael looked it up. More like two to two-and-a-half miles. In fact, years ago several NBA teams used a motion tracking software program to track how far many of their players ran. Back then, the player that ran the *farthest* per game was Luol Deng of the Chicago Bulls, who averaged 2.72 miles per game. If you figure that most of that is sprinting...

that's pretty impressive. All that said. Michael actually took his runs seriously.

They came upon two other P.E. classes running around the field. The girls were running the opposite way.

As they all passed, the guys turned their heads to check them out. Some of them were pretty cute, but Sierra wasn't in the class.

Cordell noticed several of the honey's passing and turned to Michael with a big grin on his face. Between breaths, he said, "Not bad."

"Yeah," Michael agreed, stretching his stride to keep up with Cordell's, "but not what I'm looking for."

Nick turned around and started running backward, confused. "What? You into guys now?"

"I can't quit you, Michael," Deeby jested.

Cordell laughed loud, making a spectacle, covering his mouth like the hype-man and pointing to Michael. Michael hit Deeby hard in the arm.

Deeby rubbed his arm. "You can't handle the truth."

Coach, a man who can beat any of them in any run, yelled as they were stepping out of the pack. "You guys need more running time to make up for all this horseplay?!!"

The guys knew not to respond; they just picked up the pace, resuming their spot with the group.

Finally, Michael responded to Nick's accusation. "No fool! I mean . . . the *girl* that I'm lookin' for wasn't in that pack of girls."

Cordell started smiling real big again and giggling.

"Shut up, Cordell," Michael snapped, hiding his grin, and savoring the fact that he was the only one who could actually get away with telling Cordell to shut up.

The other guys' gym class was running laps as well. Michael's weights class usually made fun of that class because... that's just the way it works. Most of the guys in weights were bigger than them. That's what it always came down to—who was bigger.

No worries. Michael thought. *If it came down to anything, I was with Cordell, that's all that mattered.*

Coach did his daily routine, dropping off after one lap to head toward the weight room ahead of us. Michael and the guys had one lap to go, then they'd join him inside.

Before long, Luke and his Neanderthal friends were messing with kids from the other P.E. class. The other class's teacher, Mr. Steel, was probably in the P.E. office reading the paper.

"Uh oh. Here it goes," Nick mumbled, nodding his head toward Luke.

Luke, Blake and the others had come up behind Brett, their favorite punching bag. And since Brett was always by himself, that made him Luke's bitch.

Homie really needs a friend.

"Apparently the girls' gym class is still out here," Luke offered, slowing his pace to match the nominal stride of Brett.

"You're right," Tyler added. "They've got a straggler here." Tyler flipped around, running backward in front of Brett, grilling him, trying to start something. "Ain't that right, bee-atch!"

Brett didn't even look up at Tyler. He just turned, staring at Luke for a long time. Michael thought Luke might have even been a little leery of that look. It kinda freaked out Michael, and he was ten feet away. Then Brett spoke as calm as his breath would allow him between strides. "My condolences on your Camaro. It's a real pity."

Cordell let out a chuckle.

Luke shot a look toward Cordell, who just stared right back. Luke was big, but he wasn't stupid.

The rest of the group was silent, aside from their heavy breathing. Half a second later, Tyler, still running backward, pounded Brett in the chest with a push so hard that Brett almost became airborne flying backward. Luke's foot was just as quick behind Brett's ankle and Brett went down hard in the muddy grass with a splat.

All of the boys jumped to the side, running around him, even his old friend Nick. None of them particularly liked what they saw, but it wasn't their fight. Brett knew that if he talked that way, he was going to get dropped. His choice.

Deeby leaned in close as we jogged away. "Crazy Carrie. Crazy Carrie."

Just another day at Mesa.

Time to lift weights.

Brett, Monday, 11:58 AM

Brett debated whether to even attend gym class today. But he didn't want to jeopardize tomorrow's plans. He'd worked too hard to blow it now with an outburst of anger. Gotta maintain control.

So long he had waited.

Only one more day.

He actually went by the office that morning to get a late slip. *Gotta be by the book for one more day.*

His run in with Luke and his little sidekicks on San Juan Avenue before school had made him twenty minutes late, but it was worth it. Because Brett was one of the only students privileged enough to see a tow truck pulling up in front of a wrecked Camaro and one very upset Luke McCormick. It was actually as if there was some force at work that had stepped in and helped Brett—at least that's what Brett told himself.

Fate's helping hand also freed him from having to endure first period with Luke. But the worst was still to come—gym class with Mr. Steel, who surely wouldn't be there in the locker room and out on the field, the two places that Luke and the other targets always seemed to find him and torment him.

But today there was something helping Brett. Brett wasn't worried about today, because the clock was ticking. As long as the sun continued to move across the sky, Luke's opportunities to continue hurting him were numbered. Physical pain was nothing because it was only temporary. Luke and all his little friends were nothing but images in the crosshairs.

Brett was in control.

Changing into his gym clothes was uneventful today. Usually Brett feared this time of day in the locker room, a particularly vulnerable time. No adults. No large crowd to blend into. No baggy street clothes to hide behind.

Brett saw no sign of Luke roaming the locker room looking for trouble. A few voices from potential threats, but no one seemed interested in picking on Brett today.

Running was tiring, as normal. Sure, none of this persecution was easy. But he could get through just one more day of this.

Voices.

The predators had arrived. Today they were predators. Soon they would be prey.

Weak people surrounded Brett. People who gathered strength from others' attention. They barked out insults, looking to gather strength. But Brett couldn't hear. Brett wasn't in the present. Brett was setting a detonator to four digits he knew all too well in his mind. Brett was looking through the scope of his AR15, safety off, exhaling slowly, preparing to gently squeeze the trigger.

More yelling.

Brett blinked twice. The images in the crosshairs disappeared.

The run was nearing the end. Brett noticed the faces around him. *Tyler and Luke. Prey.*

Brett smiled. Not only was Luke going to die tomorrow, he also just lost his prized possession. Brett almost pitied Luke. Pitied his weakness.

"My condolences on your Camaro," Brett said calmly. "It's a real pity."

Luke's face tightened up. He turned to see who was watching.

Go ahead, Brett thought. *Try to gather strength. You need it.* That's what weak people always do. They always look to see who's watching.

And the crowd always watched. Bystanders never intervened. Maybe it was fear. Maybe it was self-esteem issues. *After all, it would be social suicide to intercede for me,* Brett thought. That's why even Nick was silent. Nick had made his choice years ago.

Nick and Brett used to hang out all the time in 6th and 7th grade. He was the first friend who Brett actually opened up to about girls. Brett liked a girl named Danielle back then. He had never told anyone that but Nick. He and Nick were awake in their sleeping bags one night talking about all the girls they noticed at their middle school. Danielle was the only one in Brett's mind.

The two of them had countless memories together. Brett remembered another time when they stayed up all night binging *Stranger Things* in his room and eating Hot Pockets. They ate so many Hot Pockets Nick actually got sick.

Nick was the closest friend Brett had ever had.

Funny how things change.

Brett remembered the exact day it changed. It was in the beginning of eighth grade. He saw Nick enter the cafeteria with a bunch of football players. Nick saw Brett from across the room and gave a friendly nod. But then some of the football guys noticed Brett sitting by himself and started pointing at him. Brett never heard what they said, but he saw the struggle on Nick's face, a look Brett would always remember. He actually witnessed the dilemma going on in Nick's mind. "Should I go over and kick it with my friend Brett… *and be made fun of, too…* or should I just hang here with these guys and pretend I don't know him."

Brett remembered seeing Nick look across the cafeteria at him. He could still picture the expression on his face. Nick's look had said it all. It was as if Nick was saying, "Goodbye. Good times." And that was the end of it. Nick turned back toward the group that moment and became just another face in the crowd. The two of them hadn't spoken since.

And today was no different. Nick silently watched from the crowd of bystanders once again.

Brett didn't even see the push coming, but it didn't surprise him. He fell to the ground like a sack of grain. The grass was wet, and his body slid for a few feet in the mud. The mud was cold on his neck and arms, but it didn't matter.

Everything would be different tomorrow.

. . . tomorrow

Tuesday, 11:17 AM

He pulled the scope of his AR15 to his right eye and aimed at the students coming out the west doors. He recognized so many faces.

His finger touched the trigger. It was time. This was the moment he had been waiting for.

The crosshairs shook as his hands trembled. He regripped, trying to steady himself.

Students continued to flow out of the doors. He recognized some kids from his science class. A kid from the bus stop. He actually had sat next to him on several occasions. Never had heard him talk. The kid usually just read a book and kept to himself.

Two girls in skinny jeans, one from his gym class. A guy from his English class.

Who would be first?

He wiped his forehead and peered through the scope again. He took a deep breath and tried to convince his body to stop shaking. About ten to fifteen kids per second were getting out each set of double doors. Up to thirty kids a second, gone.

He needed to act now.

Jamie. That kid's name is Jamie.

Craig.

Dillon.

They all fled out of sight.

A cheerleader burst out of one of the doors.

I think her name is Megan. He didn't know her, but she was a cheerleader.

He squeezed the trigger.

. . . the day prior

Kari, Monday, 1:20 PM

As much as Kari enjoyed English, she hated vocabulary. *Why do you have to memorize a bunch of words?*

Mr. Hunt, Kari's 5th period English teacher, sat in the corner with his head buried in a stack of essays — last night's homework. Kari had spent almost two hours on hers. She hoped he was in an A-giving mood.

Kari looked back down at her vocabulary test. *Dictum.* What the heck was *dictum*? All Kari could remember was the jokes kids were making about it yesterday.

Kari heard the sound of Stephanie's pencil furiously filling in her Scantron bubbles on the desk next to her. Stephanie aced every one of these tests. Kari tried to, but it took a ton of time to study the words for that long. At the beginning of the year her mom used to quiz her on her list of words the night before. But once track practice started, she began hurrying a little more with her homework. Vocab was definitely an area that suffered.

Kari stared at her test. *Number seven. Dictum.* It could be any of these.

That pencil sound again.

Kari knew Stephanie had to be done with number seven by now.

She glanced at Stephanie's paper.

Yep. She's almost done. Looks like . . . she's on number 15.

She glanced at the teacher.

Kari's muscles tightened. She knew what she was about to do, but really didn't want to acknowledge it. If she acknowledged it, then she'd feel guilty. So she buried her inner moral debate.

She glanced over at Stephanie's paper again.

Seven, eight, nine . . . C, A, C . . .

She filled in the small bubbles, careful not to leave any part of the little circle empty.

But how bad was this really, Kari thought? After all, Stephanie has all the time in the world. She isn't in track, and she sure isn't going to Mexico next week to help needy kids.

It all came down to time. Kari had to choose where to spend it. And she felt like she had made good choices so far. This was one of the... *enough with that.* Stephanie was almost done. Kari knew she had better hurry.

She leaned on her hand, slyly glancing over at Mr. Hunt with her eyes, keeping her head down. He was still engrossed in essays.

Kari turned toward Stephanie's paper. *Ten, eleven, twelve, thirteen. B, C, A, D.* She sang the letters out in her head to help remember as she filled in the bubbles. *B, C, A, D.*

Twenty minutes later, just minutes before the bell rang, class might as well have been dismissed, because everyone was talking. Mr. Hunt didn't even care at this point. The class had finished going over Dostoevsky, a dreary discussion, with maddening interjections from Brett.

Now Mr. Hunt was back to his grading. He instructed the class to do silent reading, but they had learned long ago that a dull murmur was allowed within a few minutes of the bell, just not loud enough to disturb him. The class was well aware of this unwritten rule if they wanted the freedom to talk in the last few minutes. No one rocked that boat.

Stephanie continued inquiring about Kari's spring break trip. "So this is for the whole week?"

"Yeah. It's great," Kari answered. "Last year we helped rebuild a roof for this church and played with the little kids in the village. Honestly? The kids aren't used to someone playing with them or even noticing them. Many of them are abandoned... alone. So we get to just hang with them and it's just so... yeah."

The bell rang.

On the way out of the classroom Stephanie noticed Brett walking ahead of them.

"Oh my God," Stephanie whispered quietly, covering her mouth with her hand. "What does Brett have all over his ear?"

Kari looked up to see Brett walking out the door. The back of his neck was covered with something brown . . . it looked like mud or... *worse.* It was in his hair and all over his ears. *Sick.*

Some of the guys behind him were pointing at it too. Brady Edwards leaned toward him and started sniffing, then pulled away quickly, waving his hand past his nose. "Whew!"

"And I thought they smelled bad on the outside!" Deeby said. Everyone started laughing.

Stephanie turned to Kari giggling. "What is that on his neck?"

Kari held back a laugh. "I know, right? I don't even want to speculate."

Stephanie covered her mouth, cackling uncontrollably.

Kari began laughing, too, a little more relaxed since everyone else was laughing. "Bathing might be a good idea."

Stephanie laughed, and they parted ways at the door.

As Kari walked along the hallway she noticed Brett still in front of him.

Abandoned.

Alone.

She checked her phone for Snaps.

Michael, Monday, 1:20 PM

Michael didn't care for vocabulary. But it was an easy A because if he studied the words for about twenty minutes the night before, then he'd ace the test. Twenty minutes was viable, unlike math, which Michael could stare at for an hour and *still* do lousy on the test.

Michael finished his test easily then leaned back in his seat. He never liked to turn in the test right away. Didn't want to draw attention to it. Only one other kid had turned it in so far. Brianna Arthur. *Damn, that girl was smart!* In every class, too.

Michael's eyes wandered over to another group of guys on the left side of the classroom. Brady, Tyler and a couple others. They were all looking off this girl Haley's paper. If they were smart, they'd be looking at Danielle's paper to their left.

Michael looked at the group sitting in front of him. Stephanie was almost done with her test and . . . *figures.* That church girl Kari was cheating off her.

I guess she missed the "Thou shalt not cheat" week in church.

A few more people turned in their tests. Then the masses started getting up and placing their tests on Mr. Hunt's desk. Michael followed suit.

Fifteen minutes later the class was in the middle of studying Dostoevsky, the author no one could pronounce. The book was *Crime and Punishment*, and Michael found it to be intriguing. It was about this guy named Raskolnikov, a character who ends up murdering his money-grubbin' landlady with an ax. Pretty funny. Then he feels guilty about it and ends up confessing at the end. The class wasn't at the end yet, but Michael had read ahead.

Mr. Hunt was talking about the "torment" Raskolnikov was going through. This was one of those class discussions that students were supposed to be prepared for. One third of their grade was what Mr. Hunt called "class participation." That was one of the "benefits," as he always called it, of being in Honors English. He wanted to "stimulate everyone to think and express their opinions." Michael actually enjoyed these kinds of discussions back in Mrs. Allison's class. Students weren't forced to participate. She made it interesting and real, so Michael actually wanted to participate. But with Mr. Hunt, it was all a game. Michael learned quickly to find at least one opportunity to add a comment during each discussion, watching Mr. Hunt's pencil carefully. He would literally put a little check mark in his book for that day when we contributed to the discussion. Michael's friend Lance was his T.A. in 6th period. Lance would tally all the checkmarks for Mr. Hunt, who would then figure out the percentage of marks per possible days. If someone had only seventy marks out of 100 days, then they got a C in participation.

Mr. Hunt continued on, stroking his chin and pacing the floor. "Raskolnikov was plagued with guilt. His dreams haunt him, such as the dream in the end of part three where he repeatedly strikes the pawnbroker with his ax but she only laughs at him and doesn't die. How is he to be delivered from this bondage? What is the ticket to freedom here?"

Deeby raised his hand.

Mr. Hunt sighed. "Feel free to share something if you want to offer an original thought, Mr. Pearage, but I'm not interested in what Mr. Spielberg or Scorsese has to say on the matter."

Deeby slowly lowered his hand and mumbled to himself. "I'm disinclined to acquiesce to your request."

Michael raised his hand halfway. *I need my checkmark.*

"Yes, Michael."

Michael cleared his throat. "Um . . . I think that he believes that confession is the only way out. I mean, he had practically made up his mind to do it before he got distracted by saving the guy hit by the carriage. But confession was his 'ticket.'"

Mr. Hunt looked down at his book and made a little checkmark.

Aw yeah!

"Thank you, Michael. Anyone agree with that? Disagree? Anyone?"

Brett spoke up. As awkward as he was, his intelligence was undeniable. He always was reading philosophy books and quoting famous people. And who knows, maybe he wanted his checkmark, too. But this time he ranted about Raskolnikov's Christian convictions being a sign of weakness, even bringing some Nietzsche quotes to the table. Something about Dostoevsky being a victim of the self-crucifixion of two thousand years of Christianity.

Tyler turned and spoke just loud enough for half the class to hear. "Sounds like someone was the victim of two thousand years of no friends!"

The class chuckled.

"Quiet!" Mr. Hunt snapped, then quickly resumed his debate with Brett, offering some of his own Nietzsche quotes. Battle of the geeks had begun.

The class tuned out. Michael, too. Entertaining as it was, he already had his checkmark.

As the end of class finally approached, Michael gathered his books and threw them in his backpack. Only a few minutes left. He could hear Church Girl saying something about helping poor kids building a church. Ironic. *Does she cheat at church, too?*

Michael checked his phone. No texts or Snaps. *Sigh.*

He opened a new message, typed in Sierra's name with his thumbs, and stopped short. *What do I say?*

He stared at the blank box, nothing but a flashing curser, its intermittent blink reminding him he had no game.

Michael deliberated what to say to someone he'd only talked with a few times. He didn't want to be like some of the guys on the team and just type, "Hey Girl." Tisha had made it clear, "Girls don't like that stuff. Have something to say or don't say nothing at all."

Cancel

Michael put the phone in his pocket.

As Michael exited the class, people started making fun of Brett because of the mud on the back of his neck. Those in his gym class knew how it got there.

Brett didn't respond to any of their teasing. If you can handle Luke and Blake hitting you and pushing you in the mud, you can probably handle a couple of jokes from bystanders. Even Church Girl was laughing and making comments about him.

Michael shook his head. People were always baggin' on Brett. Michael felt kinda bad for him.

But it wasn't my business.

Brett, Monday, 1:35 PM

Brett tried not to think about what had just happened in gym class. It was hard to remove oneself from surrounding events, but English class served as a nice distraction. He was fascinated with the psychology in the literature they had been studying this year. Dostoevsky's *Crime and Punishment* was a nice relief from the Cro-Magnon intellect of those in gym class.

Mr. Hunt was discussing the moral struggle of Raskolnikov. Interesting, but Brett passed time thumbing through some of his favorite parts of the book. He stopped on the page where Raskolnikov planned how he would retrieve the ax for the murder. The Russian considered everything that could go wrong. "What if Nastasya walked in?"

Brett laughed to himself, identifying with Raskolnikov's line of thinking. Brett was also obsessive about his preparations.

No mistakes.

Brett's mind drifted to what he saw just last night on a CNN special about school violence, archive footage from way back of the Columbine killers and Jeff Weise from Red Lake. *Idiots,* he thought to himself. Their pride was their fall. They thought they were gods. Yet they didn't even think through the simplest problems. Maybe they should have read *this* book, Brett thought.

Eric Harris blew it three times with Columbine. First, he gave his real phone number when he ordered ammo. His dad answers the phone to hear that his ammo is in. Luckily for Harris, his dad dismissed the call as a wrong number.

Then his parents find a pipe bomb in his room. Just a hand slap. Good thing they didn't search Harris' room for more. And good thing they hadn't heard about the police report that his buddy's parents had filed, along with hundreds of pages from Harris' web site talking about the bombs he'd made. Any real D.A. would have turned that warrant in and searched Harris' place. But they didn't. *Ooops!*

And then Harris' mom caught him walking out the door with a shotgun barrel sticking out of his duffel bag. Harris told her it was a BB gun—and she bought it. *Hilarious.*

Three close calls. Never caught.

Then, to put icing on the Columbine cake, their bombs didn't go off on the big day. *Where was your backup plan for that one!* Brett thought. Harris had spent days in the cafeteria planning the perfect time to blow it up and then he screws up the fuses on the bombs. They tried for a body count of over 500 and they get just thirteen. Brett nodded slightly and clicked his tongue. *Two percent of their goal.*

And Wiese wasn't much better. *Only capped nine others before capping himself.* The sexually frustrated Carl Roberts IV did the same thing after opening fire on a bunch of Amish girls. They always shoot themselves. It's almost assumed.

He flipped a few pages further in his book. This was one of his favorite parts:

> " . . . At first — long before indeed — he had been much occupied with one question; why almost all crimes are so badly concealed and so easily detected, and why almost all criminals leave such obvious traces? He had come gradually to many different and curious conclusions, and in his opinion the chief reason lay not so much in the material impossibility of concealing the crime, as in the criminal himself. Almost every criminal is subject to a failure of will and reasoning power by a childish and phenomenal heedlessness, at the very instant when prudence and caution are most essential. It was his conviction that this eclipse of reason and failure of will power attacked a man like a disease . . ."

Brett scanned down through the paragraph. Ah, his favorite quote: *"When reason fails, the devil helps!"*

Brett didn't even notice the grin forming on his lips.

His thoughts were interrupted by something mentioned in the class discussion. His grin disappeared as he shifted his focus to what was being said. Mr. Hunt was entertaining mindless comments about how confession was good for the soul.

Brett shifted in his chair, waiting to see if anyone else was going to venture into this discussion, a subject Brett spent numerous nights thinking about.

Mr. Hunt was looking for a response. ". . . anyone? Disagree? Anyone?"

Brett was in his element. A philosophy debate on *murder and death*, no doubt —his favorite subject. It wasn't fair. No one else had a chance against him. He glanced down at his brown, homemade book cover, littered with famous quotes he had scribbled about death. Brett couldn't hold back any longer.

"I think that's where Raskolnikov shows weakness," Brett argued. "His Christian convictions are just a crutch for the weak who can't handle reality." It was a statement Brett had told himself hundreds of times.

Brett thought about stopping there, but he remembered something from Nietzsche about Dostoevsky —something he printed out the other night when he was browsing the web. "I think Nietzsche said it well . . ." Brett said, stalling, while he quickly pulled out the stapled pages from his folder, scanning the printout quickly, then stopping on the highlighted quote. "Nietzsche didn't like Dostoevsky's Christian stand and his moral convictions, either. He said that Raskolnikov was 'sinning to enjoy the luxury of confession.' He also said, 'Dostoyevsky was one of the victims of the conscience-vivisection and self-crucifixion of two thousand years of Christianity.'"

A few people mumbled something in the back of the room. The class laughed.

"Quiet!" Mr. Hunt barked, not skipping a stride. "It's funny you bring up Nietzsche," Mr. Hunt continued. "I've been researching commentary about Dostoevsky's works." Mr. Hunt seemed to enjoy the interchange. He quickly walked to his desk and shuffled through some papers, retrieving a similar printout. Scanning the paper with his finger, he stopped, removed his glasses and looked up at Brett. "Nietzsche also described Dostoevsky as the only psychologist from whom he had anything to learn.'"

Mr. Hunt put his glasses back on in triumph. "I think Dostoevsky was merely pointing out that Raskolnikov's plots didn't turn out like he planned, simply in the fact that he underestimated the power of guilt." Mr. Hunt pivoted in his wing tips, looking up as if accessing his memory banks. "I believe it was Wilson Mizner who said, 'Those who welcome death have only tried it from the ears up.'"

Brett didn't skip a beat. "Yes, but Marcus Aurelius Antoninus said,

> *"Think not disdainfully of death, but look on it with favor; for even death is one of the things that Nature wills."*

Mrs. Allison, Monday, 3:10 PM

Nancy stared at the stack of essays on the corner of her desk. *They complain about writing the essays, I'm the one who has to read almost 100 of them!*

The empty classroom was a nice break. The quiet moments after school provided a much-needed break from… *high school drama.*

Her phone vibrated on her desk.

D: U there?

Derek! I forgot to call him. Her day had slipped away from her. She had meant to call, or at least text, but her time had dissipated, and here it was already after 3 p.m.

Married life drama.

She stared at her phone debating whether to call him now, or just text him real quick and talk face-to-face later. Then she remembered. He worked late tonight. She wouldn't even see him unless he woke her up...

"You look exhausted," A voice came from behind her.

Nancy jumped, startled, dropping her phone on the floor with a clunk.

Dan Travers bent down to pick it up. "I'm so sorry. I didn't mean to scare you." He looked at the face of the phone, spider webbed, but still working. "Oh man. It's demolished."

"Oh no," Nancy investigated the phone. "Derek's gonna be so mad me. He told me to get a case for this. I kept telling him I didn't need one."

That's all I need. Something else to fight about, Nancy thought.

"Maybe you didn't need one," Dan offered with a hopeful smirk. "As long as your friend didn't sneak up behind you from the teachers' entrance. I'm sorry. It was sooooooo my bad!"

Nancy shook her head. "No, I just had one of those days." She set her phone down and picked up the stack of tests. "And it looks like I'm going to have one of those nights, too."

She began gathering her things.

"Let me walk you to your car."

"I'm fine, Dan. But thank you."

Nancy didn't mean to be cold or rude, but she really didn't want to lead Dan on either. She loved Derek. End of story... *even though she forgot to show it to him today.*

Five minutes later, Nancy was in her car, music volume up and headed home.

> *Alone*
> Heart

As she drove, she reminisced about the weekend she and Derek spent together during Christmas break. Mom and Dad had watched Gage, and the two of them escaped for just two nights in Wine Country.

Nancy chuckled as she thought about the bed and breakfast they stayed at. *Never again!* Some people like bed and breakfasts, but after this trip, she and Derek decided it would only be hotels from now on. The weekend was fun, but the bed and breakfast were far less than desirable. The shared bathrooms, the community breakfasts bursting with needy couples pouncing on any opportunity to tell you their life story. The two of them spent more time in the car that weekend than in the potpourri-scented room. They actually skipped the free breakfast on morning number two and escaped to a Denny's in Vacaville. The two of them never laughed so hard, devouring pancakes and reflecting on the weekend.

Nancy loved Derek's smile.

She drummed the steering wheel as the chorus kicked in.

> *Till now, always got by on my own. I never really cared until I met you...*

She pulled into the daycare parking lot, parked and checked her phone.

No texts from him.

She knew he worked late tonight. Tomorrow night she would make it a special night.

Kari, Monday, 7:10 PM

Kari stared at her reflection in the mirror. She didn't see what everyone else saw: captivating blue eyes with long lashes, a thin athletic frame, perfect skin... she only observed a tired little girl with frizzy hair.

She leaned closer to the mirror. *Noses are the ugliest things in the world.*

Kari dabbed the dripping water off the front of her face and looked away from her bathroom mirror long enough to slide into a comfy pair of sweats before resuming her nightly self-examination process.

What good are pores? Kari figured her nose was just one giant potential zit waiting to happen! She scrubbed it every night with the little exfoliating sponge her mom bought, and then she emerged from the bathroom looking like Rudolf the Swollen-Nosed Sophomore!

Now the computer. This would be a challenge.

Every night it was the same thing: arrive home from track in time for the family meal, watch her little brother Jordan eat more food than Kristen and her combined, watch Kristen eat less than a newborn bird, listen to Dad complain about the recent company merger, and then grab a shower to get rid of the 'I just ran seven miles' smell. After her shower, inevitably Kristen would be in the den on the computer.

Most of Kari's friends had their own laptops, but Kari's dad... who, point of fact, worked for a computer company... only bought one computer for the house. That meant when Kari wanted to work on a paper, she had to fight Kristen for the computer.

Whenever Kristen decided to actually do her homework, she typically did it on the computer. Actually, Kristen would have five other things open, three of which her parents had no clue about, and then four hours later she was finally done typing a small paragraph.

Kari grew frustrated just thinking about it.

Ain't nobody got time for that!

Typically, Kari would ask Kristen politely when she'd be finished. She usually answered something courteous like, "When I'm done. Now leave!"

Thirty minutes later Kari would ask her again if she was almost done. Many times, Kristen wasn't even looking at the computer—she was looking at her phone. But Kristen would just wave her out of the room.

That's when the normal kid would go tell Mom. But Kari's dad fixed that, because he was sick of the girls fighting over the computer every night. So he made a rule. If the girls came to him or Mom with a problem about the computer, no computer for both of them for the night. "Work it out for yourselves!" he declared.

Kristen and Kari both agreed to it . . . an agreement Kari regretted from that day forward.

Basically, Kristen grabbed the computer almost every night while Kari was in the shower and took as long as she wanted. When she finally finished taking her time, she pranced into Kari's room as if she was being thoughtful to announce the computer was free.

So tonight, Kari figured she'd just start her homework with a little Taylor Swift while waiting for the computer fairy to visit.

Shake It Off
Taylor Swift

Kari opened her phone and habitually tapped the icon she would access more than any other app throughout the day. A bunch of people had posted since she went to bed last night.

She chuckled to herself at Trevor Pribble's pic. That guy was insane.

She scrolled down through several more posts.

A guy named Jameson's broken guitar string.

Megan's cat.

Her friend Morgan's feet wearing old school Vans.

Her eyebrows wrinkled as she looked at the next post. A selfie from one of her sister's friends showing the shirt she chose that day — a particularly low-cut blouse.

Whore.

Kari set her phone down, pointed at the mirror and mimed the words as her favorite part of the song kicked in:

My ex-man brought his new girlfriend. She's like "Oh, my god!" but I'm just gonna shake...

She grabbed the history book and flipped to the page she had earmarked. She peeked ahead to see how many pages she had left. Seven. Not bad. She averaged about two minutes per page in the book.

Six minutes and three pages later Jordan bounced in. "Sissa, do you want to hear my book report?"

Kari sighed. Apparently, her face communicated the answer clearly.

"Come on, Sissa," he begged. "Look!" He turned around. "I made a prop."

He had about seven pieces of paper cut lengthwise, taped together, colored with a yellow and green crayon, and hanging out of his PJ's like a long tail.

"I have to have a prop," he said in a serious tone, his eyes fixed on Kari's.

Kari cracked a smile. Bothersome as he was, the seven-year-old was entertaining. It was better than her history homework, anyway.

"Well, what's your prop?" Kari asked.

"It's my tail. I'm a snake."

"What book did you read?"

"Verdi. It's about a python named Verdi who wants to be yellow, but he sees a green stripe on his back . . ."

"Jordan," Kari interrupted, trying to think of a way to get out of this, and still be nice. "I like your prop. It's very nice." She grabbed his little cheeks affectionately. "And I bet you're going to do great on your report. But I've gotta read these two books . . ." She fetched her Dostoevsky out of her backpack, holding it and her history book up for him to see. "...and do all my math. So why don't you see if Mom can hear it. Okay, buddy?"

Jordan turned toward the door, adjusting his tail in his pants. *Snake wedgy.* He stopped at the door. "Okay, but you would have loved the part where . . ."

"Jordan," she said quickly, stopping him from continuing on a long explanation. "You're right, I would have loved it. Maybe some other time."

The snake left her room, tail and all. She dove back into history.

An hour later the computer fairy arrived. Kari looked up from Dostoevsky.

"Computer's all yours," Kristen said.

"Well, thank you," Kari said, in the fakest possible tone she could muster.

Instead of doing her typical Vogue U-turn and exit down the catwalk, Kristen walked over to Kari's desk and started thumbing through her Mexico paperwork. Kari started to ask her what she was doing but was actually a little surprised that the Varsity cheerleader would take interest in any of her things.

"So do you really like this trip?" Kristen finally asked. Her tone was surprisingly sincere.

"I love it. It was the best week of my life last year."

Kari only had one year as a reference. But the week was life changing. She couldn't explain why. It was a week of camping in a dirty field and then driving to a little dusty village every day to play with little children. No T.V. No phone. Nasty port-a-potties. Disgusting showers.

Just you, your friends and God.

Kari never felt so close to God. *Ever.*

"Megan's going this year," Kristen continued. "She tried to talk me into going, this being my last year and all."

Kari sat silently.

"Megan is so…" Kristen searched for words… "amazing. It's like she doesn't go to church because her parents make her. She does it because she legit loves God."

Kristen looked down at the Mexico paperwork again. "Maybe I should have gone."

"Well, sign-ups ended last month," Kari quickly pointed out.

Kristen put the papers down. She seemed deep in thought. Finally, she mumbled, "Well, we have cheer practice anyway." And marched out of the room looking at her phone.

For a moment Kari felt something in her gut. *Maybe I should have…*

She glanced down at her Dostoevsky book. *I've gotta study for this exam.*

Michael, Monday, 8:35 PM

Mom and Tisha were gone for the evening. That left just Michael, his speakers, and his phone.

He turned up the volume when the beginning of the track kicked in.

> Remember the Name
> Fort Minor

He set his plate in the sink and strutted toward the couch to the beat.

This is ten-percent luck, twenty-percent skill, fifteen-percent concentrated power of will...

Michael put his hands up like a fighter and threw a few jabs at an imaginary partner.

Why is it that this song always makes me feel like getting in a fight?

Michael recognized music's power. Songs always brought distinct memories to his mind. Name it:

Thriller, MJ? Fourth grade roller rink with Emma.

Low, Flo Rida? 6th grade basketball camp.

That *Fear the Reaper* song, whoever sang it? Will Ferrell hitting a cowbell.

Plopping down on the couch, he pulled out his phone. He had an idea of something to talk with Sierra about.

His thumbs went to work.

Me: I know you're friends with Courtney.
Is she okay? Luke hit her pretty hard.

It wasn't anything ingenious... but it was something.

He stared at his phone, waiting.

Hoping.

Not three seconds later it vibrated. *Yeah boy!*

Sierra: She'll be fine. Just totally pissed off. ☺

It was on.

> **Me:** I would be too. Her car was bangin'!

> **Sierra:** Keyword. "was"

Michael laughed out loud. *Gorgeous and a sense of humor.*

> **Me:** Ha. True.

> **Sierra:** Luke actually asked her if she wouldn't call her insurance and he could just fix it.

> **Me:** Seriously?

> **Sierra:** Seriously. As if I'd let Luke touch my car!

Another text came through before Michael had a chance to reply.

> **Sierra:** ... if I had one!!!

> **Me:** Ha. I hear that. I guess my dad forgot to give me one for my birthday.

> **Sierra:** Mine too. But don't you know, all the cool kids walk to school?

> **Me:** True.

> **Sierra:** Do you and Cordell always walk to school together?

> **Me:** Every morning.

> **Sierra:** You guys seem close.

> **Me:** Like brothers.

> **Sierra:** I wish I had someone like that.

> **Me:** I'm taking applications, but I warn you, there's a waiting list. ☺

Sierra: Hahahaha. I'll give it some consideration.

A long pause.

Michael second-guessed himself. *Should I text something? Maybe I should leave it at that... not appear as if I've got nothing else to do but sit and text.*

He nestled into his mom's Cleveland Browns blanket while waiting.

Nothing.

Michael began coming to terms with the fact the conversation was over. But he considered the bright side — it was a seamless dialogue. All evidence pointed to...

His phone vibrated.

Deeby: "Beneath the clothes we find a man, and beneath the man we find his nucleus."

Michael sighed.

Me: I've got two words for you. Ther...apy.

Nancy Allison, Monday, 8:40 PM

Nancy sipped her tea without taking her eyes off her work. Only about ten tests to go.

It had been a long night. She had picked up Gage late, stopped by the grocery store, then swung by the ATM to get cash. Derek and her were trying to be good with their money and they were only spending the cash they budgeted. No credit cards.

After dinner she occupied Gage in front of a Disney movie, giving her just enough time to straighten up the house. Finally, she got him ready for bed, read him three bedtime stories, not skipping any pages, and kissed him goodnight.

Gage had only been asleep for a little while and it was back to grading tests. She took another sip of tea and set the ARMY cup on her desk. Derek had made her a cozy little office area in the corner of their bedroom. *The perks of a two-bedroom house.*

Her phone vibrated on the desk. It was Derek.

D: Hey Kiddo. Thinkin of you.

She smiled. She wished he didn't have to work late tonight. His text brightened her mood.

Nancy Pants: Thinkin of you too. How was your day.

D: Terrible without you.

Nancy Pants: You're sweet. ♡

D: Whatcha doing?

Nancy Pants: Just put Gage down for the night.
Now reading 100 Of Mice and Men tests.
Aaaaaaaaaugh!

D: Ha. I don't envy you.

She paused for a beat, putting her legs up, trying to get comfy in her desk chair. It was a shame they had fought last night and never had a chance to make up face to face. She didn't like leaving things like this.

Nancy settled for texting, for now.

Nancy Pants: I miss you.

D: Good. ☺

Nancy Pants: I was thinking we could go out tomorrow night when you get home???

D: That's sounds awesome.

Nancy Pants: I was thinking of wearing something special.

D: Cool. What?

Nancy Pants: Actually… it was something that I was NOT going to wear.

D: Oh, behave! You're going to make me come home right now!!!

Nancy Pants: Sadly, my attention is dominated by mice and men right now.

D: As long as you're wearing your underwear.

Nancy Pants: Ha. Now it's your turn to behave.

D: Never!

Nancy Pants: I really better go.

D: Awe.

Nancy waited for a moment, not sure what to type.

D: I actually have to go too. Nighty night.

Nancy Pants: Luv U!!! ♡♡♡

D: Luv you more!!!

Nancy stared at her phone for a minute.

Nothing.

With a sigh, she kicked her feet down, sat back up in her chair and reached for another test. She looked at the name. It was a bright girl from her 4th period class.

Carissa Dugan. Please wow me!

Investigator John Grove, Monday, 9:20 PM

"What you thinking about?" Manda whispered to John, gently running her fingers over his biceps. She loved his arms. They made her feel... *safe.*

John sighed. His mind was miles away.

"In-N-Out Burger."

Mandy burst out laughing. "Now you sound like a real police officer."

"Seriously though. Their fries? Animal style?" John licked his lips.

"That's not fair." Mandy said. "You can't be talking about the secret menu."

"Why not?"

"Because that's where they keep all the good stuff."

John laughed. "The Four-by-four!"

Mandy hit him playfully. "Stop! I'm getting hungry."

Mandy nuzzled into his chest.

"What are you really thinking about?"

"The job," he finally answered.

She rolled her eyes. "The job."

John gazed into her eyes, taking in the moment. Her face glowed in the moonlight. She couldn't have looked more perfect. His Marine Corps sweatshirt she loved wearing to bed was hanging off one shoulder. He reached out and touched the exposed shoulder. Her skin felt smooth and soft.

A refreshing breeze blew from the window.

Sacramento was a great place to live in the spring. The days could get into the 80s or 90s, but the nights cooled down to the low 60's because of the Delta breeze. Many residents opened their windows at night and let the fresh air cool the house.

"I'm sorry." John said. "Tomorrow's a crazy day. I've got this big bust in the morning."

"Who you busting?"

"Drug dealer named Jason Dewmore. Bad guy. Everyone's set, but it's my gig. If something goes wrong... it's on me."

Manda's forehead wrinkled. "Will something go wrong?"

John laughed. "No." He gave her a squeeze. "It's just that *if* something did... you know... the pressure is on."

John got lost in thought for a moment.

Manda married John while he was still in the Corps. They lived in base housing for the first year. Then John was deployed to Kuwait for six months for some Desert Storm aftershocks. John never shared the details, but he came back... *different.*

John wasn't uber-emotional before Kuwait, but afterward, he was a lockbox. Manda had spent years desperately searching for the key. It wasn't until about a decade later that he began opening up, a recollection here and there. Small stories, memories that made Mandy shudder just to think about.

No wonder he's quiet about these memories.

But talking was better than locking it away and pretending it wasn't there... at least that's what Manda heard Dr. Phil say. So the two of them began talking about their feelings more consistently: work, finances... vivid memories of friends lost during those six horrific months.

Manda was a good listener. That's probably why they grew to be more than just spouses or lovers. They were truly best friends. She knew when to let him talk, and more importantly, when to let it go.

She grabbed his hand and kissed it.

"You've always done good under pressure," she assured him. "It's one of your amazing qualities."

"Ha. I'm glad I've got you fooled."

She leaned forward and kissed him gently on the lips.

"Everything should be fine," he continued, possibly trying to comfort Manda, but more likely trying to assure himself. "I've done my homework, and Jorgy's SWAT team is really good at what they do."

He looked away. "But it's just..." John left the thought unfinished.

"It's just *the job.*" Manda finished for him.

John nodded agreement. "It's just the job."

Manda snuggled up closer to him. "Yeah, but when you're done with the job tomorrow you get to come home to your smoking hot wife and then you can forget about the job."

"True."

She kissed him delicately on his neck, moving up to his ear, then paused again.

"I know you're good at what you do..." Manda searched for the right words.

"I sense a big 'but' approaching." John said.

Manda sat up and crossed her arms, feigning offense. "Who's got a big butt?"

John put his arms around her. "You! You've got a big ol' Beyonce butt."

Manda frowned. "Has that line ever worked for you?"

John laughed. "Not really, but I couldn't think of anything else. Give a brutha some slack."

John kissed her softly on the lips. Manda played a little hard to get, but eventually accepted his advances.

An hour later Manda was fast asleep. John lay awake, staring at the ceiling.

What were you doing at that house, kid?

Brett, Monday, 9:30 PM

"Well, don't expect me to wash your clothes."

She bought it.

This night didn't seem any different. *It was so easy to lie to his mom,* Brett thought, throwing his soiled gym-class clothes on top of the washing machine and heading toward his room upstairs. He had been lying to her for years.

Mud football with my friends.

As far as she knew, he had a ton of friends. Although, Brett couldn't help but wonder how she could have possibly missed some of the obvious signs that this wasn't the case:

> *1. No one ever comes over. Don't you realize that if I had friends they'd come over? Ever think of that? Or are you too busy working late at dad's office to even notice!*

> *2. No one ever texts me. But you wouldn't know what I do on my phone anyway.*

> *3. I never go out. No school dances. No football games. No parties. I just sit here rotting in my effing computer chair, chatting online with imaginary friends that probably have pathetic lives just like me!*

Brett closed the door to his room, locking the deadbolt. He had added the deadbolt to his door nine months ago. It took his parents three months to notice. His dad told him to remove it, but Brett ignored him. That usually worked. His parents never followed through on anything.

He plopped in his all-too-familiar spot in front of the computer, entered his password, and routinely placed his earbuds in each ear.

Silence.

Open playlist, and play.

Du Hast
Rammstein

Brett paused and closed his eyes for a moment, tilting his head back as the music poured into his veins.

Du, du hast. Du hasst mich...

Brett didn't know German, but he knew what these guys were singing: *You hate me!*

As his eyes opened, he felt alive and focused.

His fingers navigated the keyboard quickly and effortlessly. He scanned several sites for messages, his favorite social media pit stops. Within minutes he was back on a web site that was a frequent landing of late. The page featured research and statistics about past school shootings. Brett's thoughts about Columbine earlier in the day whet his appetite for further study of what mistakes were made. Brett scrolled down the page, stopping to read something that caught his eye. He opened his journal and jotted down some notes.

Brett thought that this Scottish guy deserved some attention. In 1996 he killed sixteen kids and one teacher. *Eat that Harris.* Brett read further. Sure enough, he killed himself just like the others.

Brett scanned down the page. In Yemen a guy killed eight people at two schools. But yeah, Brett thought. *Duh! Yemen!*

Brett giggled to himself at the next entry. "Two students killed and seven wounded by Luke Woodham, sixteen, who was also accused of killing his mother." *Not a bad idea,* Brett thought.

Brett hit his arrow key, moving down a few notches on the page. *This was interesting.* "Four students and one teacher killed, ten others wounded outside as Westside Middle School emptied during a false fire alarm. Mitchell Johnson, thirteen, and Andrew Golden, eleven, shot at their classmates and teachers from the woods."

Brett liked their thinking. Although he planned on doing better than a "false" fire alarm.

Brett's eyes continued skimming down the page, stopping at the section on Columbine. Brett sat up for a second and stroked his chin. He hit the arrow up and scanned the entries pre-Columbine. Then he hit the down arrow and looked post Columbine.

Holy...

Columbine had catalyzed something. Maybe it was the press—a chance to be famous. Brett wondered if maybe the event just solidified an existing idea in these teenager's brains. Whatever it was, shortly after the April 20, 1999 Columbine shooting, the occurrences increased dramatically:

> April 28, 1999
> Taber, Alberta, Canada
> Just eight days after Columbine. One student killed, one wounded at W. R. Myers High School in first fatal high school shooting in Canada in 20 years. The suspect, a 14-year-old boy, had dropped out of school after he was severely ostracized by his classmates.

> May 20, 1999
> Conyers, GA
> One month after Columbine. Six students injured at Heritage High School by Thomas Solomon, 15, who was reportedly depressed after breaking up with his girlfriend.

Brett scanned down the page. November, another one. December, two more. Then March... *interesting*:

> March 5, 2001
> Santee, CA
> Two killed and 13 wounded by Charles Andrew Williams, 15, firing from a bathroom at Santana High School.

March 7, 2001
Williamsport, PA
Elizabeth Catherine Bush, 14, wounded student
Kimberly Marchese in the cafeteria of Bishop
Neumann High School; she was depressed and
frequently teased.

March 22, 2001
Granite Hills, CA
One teacher and three students wounded by Jason Hoffman, 18, at Granite Hills High School. A
policeman shot and wounded Hoffman.

"Wow. Three in one month." Brett whispered to himself.

He scrolled down and stopped once again at a listing he was
really familiar with: Laguna Creek High School. Laguna Creek
was thirty minutes from Brett's house.

February 11, 2004
Authorities charged two 15-year-old boys with
conspiring to murder their classmates at Laguna
Creek High School. The boys — one a freshman,
the other a sophomore — were arrested after another student's parent tipped law enforcement officials that the pair were plotting to attack Laguna Creek High with guns and bombs. Both are
charged with two counts each of conspiracy to
commit murder and one count of attempted burglary.

Brett giggled at their carelessness. "Don't blab before you do
it!" he scolded the screen before scrolling down to some more
recent dates, landing on one he remembered his parents watching on the news.

April 9, 2014

> 16-year-old Alex Hribal went on a rampage at his high school in Murrysville, Pennsylvania, stabbing or slashing 20 students and a security officer. Interviewed months later, Hribal told doctors "He witnessed bullying that upset him, so he wanted to make the world a better place."

Brett laughed. "I agree!"

But his laugh soon faded as he navigated to a picture of a group of small kids being led by a teacher to safety. Sandy Hook. Twenty-seven killed. Kids. Young kids.

What could they have possibly done?

Brett quickly clicked another link to the Florida shooting from early 2018. Seventeen killed, and the shooter was actually arrested. Almost unheard of.

Brett leaned in close to the screen as a sentence caught his attention.

...concealed himself in the crowd fleeing the school...

He clicked another link and read more about the shooter.

Ostracized.

Bullied.

"No shit. Wake up, America!"

And sure enough, after the Florida shooting there were countless aftershocks of school violence: Palmdale, Santa Fe, Noblesville...

Bored, Brett scrolled to the top of the page and read the first entry again. He was staring at one of the least-publicized school massacres but yet the most successful. The worst school attack in the history of the U.S. occurred in 1927 when a farmer, angry about school taxes, blew up a school in Bath, Michigan, killing forty-five. Well... worse school attack. Vegas was a whole nother story.

"Vegas!" Brett sighed, leaning back in his chair.

Molly raised her head from the corner of the room as if to check if Brett was talking to her. Brett heard her collar jingle and tapped his leg. Molly quickly obliged, getting up from her comfy spot in the corner and sat on the floor immediately next to Brett where she received her favorite reward, a behind-the-ears scratching.

Molly was Brett's Golden Retriever, and currently, his only friend. Brett had saved Molly's life, and Molly just might have saved his. After a particularly hard day in junior high, Brett was riding his dad's bike across the old red footbridge in Fair Oaks. Brett wove past a few fisherman and started to shift into a higher gear when a little girl holding a puppy stopped him.

"Do you want a puppy?" she had pleaded, holding out the puppy as he rode by.

Brett slammed on his breaks, which squealed loud enough to scare away all the fish for miles. The little girl handed him the puppy, immediately telling him a sad story of how she was going to have to throw the puppy over the side of the bridge if she couldn't find someone to take it. Brett listened to the tale, not knowing how true it was, and not really caring. The furry little panting face seemed relaxed with Brett—safe.

"Her name is Molly," the little girl said.

Brett held the puppy up, looking into the puppy's eyes. Molly licked his nose.

Puppy breath.

Before giving it another thought, Brett had agreed to take the puppy. He tucked her away in his father's front handlebar bag he zipped almost completely closed, except a small hole that the puppy poked her tiny head out in no time at all. Once home, Brett relayed the story to his parents, who immediately insisted he get rid of it. After days and eventually weeks of threatening to take the puppy to the pound, his parents tired of the daily battle and let him keep the dog. "But it's your responsibility!" they asserted. "You feed it. You clean up its mess. You do everything. And the moment it tears anything up, it's history!"

It. They always called *her* "it."

Brett agreed to their demands—anything to keep her. He would have agreed to cutting off his arm if that's what it took. And the friendship emerged—Brett and Molly.

Knock knock.

Someone was at Brett's door. Probably his mom. It didn't happen often, but whenever it did...

"Just a second."

Brett ran to his computer and pulled up Spotify. He quickly called up a playlist called Manchurian, cuing up Journey's song *Faithfully* halfway through and hitting play. He unplugged his earbuds and slowly turned up the volume until Journey emerged from the speakers. He set Christopher Cross's *Sailing* next in the queue.

Brett unbuttoned his pants and unbolted his door.

"Come in."

Brett buttoned his pants as she walked in. "Sorry, I had to get dressed."

"It's fine," she said. "I'm going to bed. I just wanted to tell you that I put your gym clothes in the wash. But next time if you get them dirty, throw them in the laundry room deep sink with a little laundry soap. That way the stains won't set in. You don't want to look like one of those apartment kids."

"Okay," Brett nodded. "I will next time."

Brett smiled, hoping she would leave, and bring her dictionary definition of classism with her.

No such luck.

Arms crossed she looked around the room, tapping her lip with her finger, powerless to mask her disdain. "You aren't always going to have someone doing your laundry you know. If you ever want to be successful..."

Almost as if on cue, *Faithfully* crossfaded into *Sailing*. Brett's Mom paused, entranced by the melodic introduction of the strings.

"Oh!" She sighed, closing her eyes. "This song is amazing."

Within two measures of the hypnotic guitar riff, she was spellbound.

Brett held his smirk.

Sailing was catnip for parents. Brett learned this two years ago at his aunt's Christmas party, a horrific event overall, but where he first observed how easy it was to alter the moods of grown-ups using music. It's remarkable more teenagers haven't noticed this. His cousin Emily had just been caught filling her glass from the adult punchbowl when *Sailing* came through the speakers. Everyone was entranced, not unlike when Andy Dufresne played opera through the prison speakers at Shawshank.

If you ever want to brainwash Mom and Dad, just put on Christopher Cross. He's crack cocaine for parents. They'll forgive all your transgressions and double your allowance.

His mom turned towards the door. "You've got great taste in music Brett, I'll give you that."

Brett manufactured a smile. "I learned from the best."

She closed the door behind her. He wouldn't see her the rest of the night.

Brett hit his spacebar killing Christopher Cross, walked over to his bookshelf and reached behind the books on the second shelf pulling out a folded piece of binder paper.

> *420*
>
> *6:00*   *get up*
>
> *6:10*   *load Tahoe—get out*
>
> *Dead time—check gear*
>
> *10:40*   *arrive Cabrillo—set up decoy*
>
> *10:48*   *set 15-minute delay*
>
> *10:58ish*   *arrive at school*
>
> *Gear up! (35 seconds)*

11:00	*drop gear at perch—grab device*
11:02	*place device in Cafeteria—set timer*
11:03	*Park fun begins*
11:04ish	*Cabrillo 911 call. (4 to 8 minute response time in October.)*
11:08	*lunch bell*
filler up!	
11:17	*BOOM. Playtime! (9 minutes until first officer—14 minutes before SWAT dispatched- 33 minutes until authorized to go in)*

Brett reviewed the times in his head several times. Then he copied the schedule from memory on a piece of paper to test himself. He didn't miss a mark.

Ripping up the paper into pieces and tossing them in the garbage, he let the dog out of the room, locking the deadbolt behind her.

"You don't want to see this, girl."

He slid a duffle bag out from under his bed, unzipped it and arranged the contents on the floor: guns, timers, several bricks of M100s, and another device that he handled extra carefully.

The M100s might have been overkill. In his tests in the woods the M80s seemed plenty loud, but the M100s were truly deafening. But deafening was probably an accurate word to describe the sound of an AR15 rifle. Television speakers can't possibly prepare you for how painfully loud a gun truly is in person, especially one like this. That's why he chose the M100s for the park. *Had to sound convincing.*

He set the M100s aside and picked up his AR15. He had cleaned and lightly lubricated it Saturday when his parents were gone. The YouTube video was pretty detailed about the importance of lubricating the gun effectively. Brett followed the instructional video to the last detail.

He tried popping in the magazines without looking. He had multiple thirty-round magazines taped together, head to toe, in pairs. Thirty-round magazines were illegal in California, but that didn't keep people from driving them in from out of state.

Same with his Glock. The 9MM had a perfectly good seventeen-round magazine, but stupid California only allowed the ten-round single stack version. So he had to spend some good money to get one from out of state. Illegal always costs more money.

Brett set the AR15 aside and picked up his shotgun, a semiautomatic 12-gauge equipped with an extended magazine that held six rounds. Some criminals preferred the sawed-off. But that was usually so you could conceal it. There would be no concealing what Brett was going to do tomorrow. And the barrel's length wasn't much longer than the extended magazine, which stuck out a lot further, so you can pack in six rounds, plus one in the chamber. Brett knew he'd be a lot happier only having to reload after seven shots, as opposed to five. Once seven shots were fired, he'd simply flip it over, load six shells underneath and one in the chamber. Cycle the action once and you're ready to go. No pumping necessary.

Gotta love semiautomatic.

Sure, it doesn't make that cool pumping sound that scares the piss out of people, but it would be ready to fire when he needed it.

Brett's TV caught his attention—some movie on cable. A man's Lexus broke down and some gangsters stopped and were hassling him. Danny Glover showed up in a tow truck and started helping the guy with the broken-down car, ignoring the gang bangers.

Brett looked up the movie on his phone really quick. Brett liked looking up movies and seeing who wrote them, directed them, etc. This movie was called *Grand Canyon*. How come he had never heard of it?

One of the bangers confronted Danny Glover:

Gangbanger: Do you think I'm stupid? Just answer that question first.

Glover: Look, I don't know nothing about you, you don't know nothing about me. I don't know if you're stupid or some kind of genius. All I know is that I need to get out of here, and you got the gun. So I'm asking you for the second time, let me go my way here.

Gangbanger: I'm gonna grant you that favor, and I'm gonna expect you to remember it if we ever meet again. But tell me this, are you asking me as a sign of respect, or are you asking because I've got the gun?

Glover: Man, the world ain't supposed to work like this. I mean, maybe you don't know that yet. I'm supposed to be able to do my job without having to ask you if I can. That dude is supposed to be able to wait with his car without you ripping him off. Everything is supposed to be different than it is.

Gangbanger: So what's your answer?

Glover: You ain't got the gun, we ain't having this conversation.

Gangbanger: That's what I thought, no gun, no respect. That's why I always got the gun.

Brett chuckled to himself. *Exactly.*

PART III

"And in the end, it's not the years in your life that count. It's the life in your years."

-Abraham Lincoln

Investigator John Grove, Tuesday, 5:58 AM

John took a final swig from the Dasani water bottle, pouring the last few drops in his hand and wiping it on his face. Glancing at his watch, he raised the small radio to his lips, "Only two minutes, fellas."

He watched as Jorgy's team moved into place. Brian Jorgenson was an ex-Delta commando although John thought he should have been a Marine. Some say Deltas are far superior, but John had a lot of jarheads in the family and liked the Corps.

Jorgy probably slept with his MP-5; he sure cleaned it enough.

John wouldn't want anyone else watching his back. Jorgy's team had done this kind of infiltration a thousand times. This raid would be a walk in the park. Their goal was to bag Dewmore and Jeremy Fullberry and collect everything they could to put them away for a long time.

John woke up night after night in a cold sweat with the vivid pictures of Bobby Armitage, Brian Scott, and Carrie Reid burned in his head. All three were under fifteen. All three were victims of senseless shootings with weapons that Dewmore's little enterprise had provided. John loved kids, and he had a hard time watching them get slaughtered so that Jason Dewmore could get new 24-inch rims for his Escalade.

John checked the magazine on his 9MM Beretta, and quietly exited the rusted Cutlass. He had done this long enough to know that typical unmarked 4-door sedans were like neon signs in this neighborhood. Officers loved rollin' in agent Grier's 1996 Oldsmobile Cutlass. It looked like a drug dealer's car but handled like a cop car.

Everyone was in place. The only sound was that of a distant plane taking off. It was six a.m. No one in this neighborhood would be up for hours. They only went to bed… passed out, that is… a few hours ago.

John nodded to Jorgy, and Jorgy said something into his headset. All at once his team moved. The entry points were the front door and the rear slider. It was already confirmed that the rear slider was unlocked, and "Mr. Knock Knock" would take care of the front door, no problem. Mr. Knock Knock was the team's nickname for the battering ram that had granted them access to hundreds of dealer nests just like this one.

John touched his inside pocket, running his fingers over the warrant, an obsessive habit of his after seeing what had happened to one of his buddy's cases when he had neglected that step.

The sound of Mr. Knock Knock splintering the door sent everyone's adrenaline through their bloodstreams. The team was in the house in seconds with guns poised and reflexes sharp. John followed Jorgy, another old habit that John didn't particularly want to dismiss. The old floor creaked as they entered the kitchen. The yellowing, badly stained linoleum was peeling in every corner, not to be outdone by the smoke-stained dingy gray carpeting.

A young kid with braids popped up from the couch only to be staring down the barrel of an MP-5. He made a quick glance at the sliding glass door, but all hope faded from his face when he saw another blue uniform outside pointing the same weapon of choice at his head. John didn't recognize this individual. But it was common for people to kick it at the Dewmore house for the night. And this guy was faded on something.

John followed Jorgy down the hall into the left bedroom, Dewmore's lair. By now the team had covered every square inch of the house. John relaxed his right arm, but with a firm grip on his Beretta. Dewmore was standing by the bed with a blanket wrapped around him. His girlfriend was yelling at Jorgy's man. Might as well have yelled at the Lincoln Memorial—he didn't even blink.

Only when Dewmore made a move for his pants on the ground, did Jorgy's man move. He closed his distance by three feet, not saying a word, just nodding his head and clicking his tongue. Dewmore's expression was priceless. John enjoyed seeing fear on his face. No matter how tough people tried to be on the street, staring down an MP-5 in a trained hand had an effect on them.

Dewmore's girlfriend was badmouthing Jorgy's team member. Jorgy moved his massive frame a step further into the room and just looked at her. Everything drained from her face . . . she had nothing left to say. She just sunk her body deeper into the bed sheets, while keeping her hands in the air for Jorgy's guy.

As she silenced, John heard somebody rambling in the other room. John gave Dewmore a wink and stepped out of the bedroom toward the second door.

And what was behind door number two?

Two of Jorgy's men were in this room with their weapons aimed on two young black males. John recognized one as Jeremy Fullberry. Two females huddled in the corner as well. One was crying while the other just stared at Jorgy's men, as if in a trance. One of Jorgy's men yelled, "Hands!" to the fidgety male next to Jeremy. He was mumbling to himself and looking around for any way out of the room.

Fullberry yelled, "Shut up!"

"Fidgety" just kept moving like a scared dog trapped in an ally. Jorgy's man had him and didn't seem too worried about the 140-pound brother standing there in his boxers.

He mumbled some more, "I knew dat we shouldn't of... I knew dat boy was trouble ..."

Fullberry yelled again, "Shut the ..."

Jorgy's man yelled, "Hey!" and took a step toward Jeremy. And that's when the fidgety one must have lost it. He sprung toward the window and jumped through the glass, landing in the bushes outside. John's gun sprung up and Jorgy's man hesitated on his trigger.

John knew he was losing one of his witnesses, the kind he liked, the jittery talkity type. He couldn't wait to get this guy into an interrogation room.

Jorgy's man with a gun on Fullberry never moved, but the other man followed John to the window. John started to leap out the window himself but relaxed when he saw two of Jorgy's men come from each side in the backyard. They grabbed the bleeding window-hopper out of the bushes, threw him on his stomach, and had him in cuffs before he hit the ground.

John walked back through the hall, smiling as he passed the room where Dewmore was being cuffed. He exited the back-slider and walked over to the jittery one, who had been stood up and was being escorted to the back patio area, if you could call it that. A small island of cracked cement rested in the middle of the knee-high weeds covering the back yard. John waited until he was read his rights. He didn't want to mess that one up.

As "Fidgety" entered the sidewalk he looked at John and started nodding his head back and forth. "I knew dat white boy was trouble. I told dem not to deal with him. What's a cracka doin' in the hood! Bringing Five-O is what he's doin'." Jorgy's man escorted him around the side toward the front yard. John followed and decided to play with the suspect.

"Yep. Brought us right to you." John said, fishing.

The suspect dropped his head. "I knew it. I should have dropped him, know what I'm saying?" He spit some blood from his mouth and licked his bleeding lip.

John tried something. "Yeah—I figured you knew something was up. So why did you deal with him? You're smarter than that."

"I didn't," he announced, looking from side to side and then lowering his voice. "Those niggas did," motioning his head toward the house. "I knew he wasn't fo real."

"Yeah," John continued. "But why would they want to turn away a good customer who's looking for a little sum sumtin'. Besides, if he's got the chips ..."

"I don't care how he was rollin'. I wouldn't have helped dat white boy tool up for nothin'."

Jorgy's guy looked up at John confused.

John's face changed. *Tool up? Guns? I thought this was just some white kid looking for some meth, not guns.*

Could this be the kid that Hicks followed?

Fidgety noticed the surprise on John's face and looked away. He realized he had said too much.

Jorgy poked his head outside the front door, "Grove! You're going to want to see this."

John held up his hand to Jorgy, motioning for him to hold on a second. But it looked like Fidgety was done. He was looking at the front door. Dewmore was being escorted out the doorway, and one look from him silenced John's new gabby friend. Sharing time was over.

John followed Jorgy inside to the hallway. A ladder was set up underneath the attic access. John took just a few steps up the ladder and smiled. Not the smartest group he'd come up against. Shotguns, semiautomatic rifles, Mac 10s and .22-caliber handguns all stacked on a sheet of plywood laid across the insulation.

"I don't think we have to worry about making a conviction stick," John said.

But John wasn't totally relieved when he went down the ladder. *What does a white suburban boy want with these guys? Why would he want guns?*

That kid was the only white boy John knew about visiting this neighborhood. It was his only lead. But John couldn't deal with that right now. This bust meant paperwork.

Kari, Tuesday, 7:05 AM

Three taps of the snooze again before she got up, but no concern. She had showered the night before and she somehow arrived at the bathroom before Kristen again. Two days in a row. Maybe it was a sign—*today might turn out to be a good day.* Mom was already at the breakfast table when she arrived. "Good morning sweetheart. Want me to make you something?"

"Oh, that's sweet, Mom, but no. I think I'll just go for something healthy again this morning." Kari grabbed a box of Cocoa Puffs as she said it, smiling.

"Are you sure?" her mom asked. "It would be no problem for me to whip up some eggs really quick."

"Thanks, but I'm fine. Cocoa Puffs are one of the bright moments of my day," Kari confessed. "Plus, I'm not really worried about the calories when I'm running in gym class and then for two hours in track after school. I might just have a bagel and cream cheese to top it all off."

"Ha! I remember those days," Mom said. "Of course, now if I even *think* about cream cheese I gain three pounds on my thighs." She grabbed the side of her thighs and sighed.

Kristen glided into the room. "You really shouldn't talk like that, you know, Mom. Mrs. Surrel actually told us about a study that says your mom's self-esteem affects your self-esteem. If moms are always worried about their weight and stuff, then we'll be worried about our weight."

Kristen peeled a banana and took a bite.

"Well, I guess you guys are going to be all messed up then," her mom quipped, not even looking up from her paper. "Because I'm fifteen pounds overweight and already scared of what I'm going to look like in my shorts this weekend. Wow!" She set her paper down. "Can you believe it's already shorts weather?"

Kristen rolled her eyes. "Yeah. Like four weeks ago."

"If I had your legs, I'd probably have been wearing shorts four weeks ago, too!" Kari offered spitefully.

Kristen threw her banana peel away and curtsied. "Why, thank you." Her fake smile evaporated. "Let's get!"

Kari and her mom looked at each other. Kari rolled her eyes. "Must be nice," Mom said.

"I guess that's my cue," Kari said, kissing her mom on the cheek, tossing her bowl in the sink and adding a skip to her step so she didn't miss her ride. Kristen definitely *would* leave Kari in a heartbeat.

Michael, Tuesday, 7:20 AM

Tisha and Mom must have been running late this morning, because Michael didn't see a sign of them during breakfast.

He flopped on the couch and pulled out his phone, fixin' to Airplay some music before heading to Cordell's.

Two Texts

Hmmmm. *Could it be Sierra?*

> **Cordell:** You left your Jersey at my house. Nana washed it. I'll bring it to school today.

> **DB:** I didn't do my Algebra again. Sometimes I Have the feeling I can do crystal meth, but then I think, mmm... better not.

No Sierra.

Mom walked into the kitchen, glancing Michael's way. "What you so stressed about?"

"Stressed? I look stressed?"

Mom put her hand on her hip. "*Hmmmm.* Let me guess. A girl?"

"Ha! I wish. I mean, yeah, I guess I was hoping to get a text from *said girl.*"

"No texts?"

"Just from Cordell and DB."

"Deeby?" Mom asked. "Is that the white boy who's always talkin' 'bout movies?"

"That's the one."

Mom shook her head and exhaled. "Something's wrong with that boy."

Michael chuckled to himself just thinking of him.

"So what's the girl's name?" Mom asked, pouring coffee in a thermos.

"Sierra."

"I don't think I've heard you talk about her before. She someone new in your life?"

"Not really," Michael answered, tossing his phone on the coffee table and putting his feet up. "We just started texting recently."

"You like her?"

"Yeah."

"What you like about her?"

"Besides the fact that she's fine? I don't know. She's pretty
cool."

"Ha, both fine and cool." Mom sipped her coffee and licked
her lips. "Well remember that *fine* don't last. *Cool* does. So make
sure she's more *cool* than *fine*."

Michael smiled. Some people's moms don't know much, but
Michael's mom was smart. Street smart. Sadly, she learned a lot
of her lessons at the school of hard knocks. *Thanks, Dad.*

"Can the two of you talk easily?" Mom asked.

"You mean *talk* talk? Like face to face?" Michael asked.

"Yeah. Not through that stupid thing," she said, sitting down
next to him and pointing to his phone.

"Hey, you bought me this '*stupid thing.*' And you like being
able to reach me whenever."

"True," Mom said. "But don't misunderstand me. That thing
is a good supplement to communication in a relationship, but
it's a lousy replacement. Make sense?"

"Yeah. It's a good addition to existing communication. But if
you only communicate on the phone, you miss out."

"Exactly," she smiled. "When did you get so smart?"

"Birth! Some cats got it, some cats don't."

She laughed at that and hugged him. "Well, you got it."

Michael sat for a moment in her arms, unaffected by the silence.

"Mom?"

"Yeah, baby?"

"How do you know when you've met someone... you
know..."

"Special?"

"Yeah. You know."

"Well," she said, leaning back on the couch. "When the two of you talk and you never want the conversation to be over. Time just passes."

Michael jumped off the couch. "Time! I gotta finish getting ready. Nana will kill me if I make Cordell late."

She kissed him. "I love you, Michael!"

"Love you too, Momma."

Nancy Allison, Tuesday, 7:20 AM

"Come on, Gage, eat your..." Nancy picked up the jar and read the label. "...sweet potatoes." Nancy tilted her head to the side. "Hmmm. I like sweet potatoes."

Gage watched as Nancy cautiously tried a bite of his baby food.

Her eyebrows raised. "*Mmmm*. Not bad."

Instead of feeding Gage, she finished off the jar.

Derek strolled in dressed in his gray micro twill pants, and a royal blue fitted MX dress shirt from Express, one of Nancy's favorite stores.

"Wow. Stealing food from a baby," he said. "Literally."

Nancy laughed. "Caught me." She leaned out to give him a kiss as he walked by. "What time did you get in last night?

"About 11:30. You were zonked."

"I bet. After grading 100 tests I was done... *with life!* Sacked about 10:30."

Derek poured himself a bowl of cereal and began his process of stirring the cereal in the milk with his spoon, making sure each little Golden Graham was submerged indiscriminately.

He looked up from his bowl. "I was kinda hoping you'd be up."

Nancy washed out the jar in the sink and dropped it in the recycle bin to her left. She walked over to Derek's chair and wrapped her arms around him from behind. "Tonight," she whispered.

They kissed for a moment but then stopped short in the silence. They looked over at Gage's high chair. He was just sitting there entranced, watching them.

They burst out in laughter.

"We should try this more often," Derek suggested. "I've never seen him behave so well."

Nancy looked at the clock on the wall and began to pull away. "I've gotta go."

Derek whimpered like a puppy. "Really? You don't have just a minute?" He posed his best cute and cuddly look.

Nancy giggled. "Sorry, Puss in Boots. You look amazing, but I'm truly going to be late." She gave him a peck on the lips and pulled away.

"To be continued tonight," Derek said.

Nancy grabbed her purse and her school bag. "Tonight. Wouldn't miss it for the world."

Kari, Tuesday, 8:05 AM

"Pass your homework up," Mr. Colfax chimed routinely.

Every day it was the same thing in first period. It was so monotonous it was inebriating.

Kari wasn't alone in her sheer boredom. Everyone else looked as lethargic as her. Even Deeby was refraining from his normal movie banter.

Hmmmm. The chair in front of Misty was empty once again. Two days in a row of no Brett.

No loss.

Two seconds later the empty seat was forgotten.

Mrs. Allison, Tuesday, 8:20 AM

"Don't worry," Nancy assured her class, handing them back their essays. "Overall I felt you did really well. I felt like many of you have a good understanding of the book. My bigger concern was your composition. So we're going to spend a little time talking about that today."

She walked up to the whiteboard and began to write. The blue dry-erase marker barely worked. Nancy threw it in the garbage and searched for another. They weren't in her top drawer…

Nancy remembered that she had one in her purse. No surprise. Derek constantly teased her about how much she carried in her purse.

When are you every going to need a dry erase marker? He would say.

She searched through her purse. It wasn't in the main pocket. *Side pocket.* Must be there.

She glanced in her side zipper pocket and froze, cursing under her breath.

Her eyes darted up to see if her students were watching her. Most had used the opportunity to tune out and check their phones.

She swallowed hard and tried to act casual. Her Smith & Wesson Bodyguard 380 was in that side pocket—she had forgotten to take it out in the rush this morning.

She had never done that. Nancy knew better. All concealed carriers knew better than taking their weapons to a school. But last night she habitually grabbed it out of her lockbox by the bed when she went shopping and to the ATM.

Nancy got the gun as soon as she became a civilian. Several of her old MP friends had gone with her to get their carrying permits, too. Nice to have, but never needed it.

She zipped the pocket closed quickly. No one would ever know.

Aha!

Black dry-erase marker, side snap pocket.

Investigator John Grove, Tuesday, 9:45 AM

John stepped out of the station to get some fresh air. The morning had gone well, but he was still bothered by the reference to the "white boy." Franklin Williams, the suspect who was so happy to talk in his boxers at the Dewmore place, was a mute at the police station. John didn't hear another peep about a "white boy."

John got in his car before he realized that he didn't know where he was going. He pushed speed dial number four on his cell phone. Bixler answered — just who he was hoping for.

"Bixler, it's Grove."

"Hey Grover. Done bagging your boy yet?"

"Hopefully, but I gotta look into something else," John said, changing the subject. "Quick favor — can you look in my in-box for a manila folder with a kids name on it in red pen. Last name Colton . . . I think."

"Hold on," Bixler said.

John could hear Bixler setting the phone down to walk over to his desk. Bixler was a good investigator. Everyone on the force liked him.

John started his car. He liked his Crown Vic much more than Grier's Cutlass.

He pulled out of the driveway, not knowing where he was going . . . *yet,* but started to head toward Carmichael. He knew it was somewhere in Carmichael.

Bixler came back on the phone. "Brett Colton — I got it right here. What do you need?"

"I need a home address."

John could hear Bixler thumbing through the folder. "Bingo," Bixler said. "419 Shady Elm Drive."

"I'm driving. Can you . . ."

"Already on it," Bixler interrupted. "Just texted it to you."

"Thanks a million, Bix."

"No problem, Grover."

"Hey," John added. "Some really entertaining reading in the back of that file. Hicks got his ass kicked by a lady." John smiled.

Bixler laughed. "I think I just might have to read that. See ya, Grover."

John clicked the address on the text and began following the soothing female voice's directions. This whole venture was a shot in the dark, but it could be interesting.

Brett, Tuesday, 10:37 AM

In forty minutes it would begin.

He had traveled this road overlooking Cabrillo Park countless times, but never in this vehicle, and never with such focus. The park was just nine minutes from his school. He had timed it repeatedly.

Brett carefully pulled the SUV to a stop in the shadows of a prune tree, shifting the vehicle in park, and letting the engine idle...

Not even five minutes later Brett walked over to the barricade up on the hill overlooking the serene little park. His gaze swept across the children playing on the swings below. *Too young for school. Lucky.*

Taking a deep breath, he hit the start switch on his timer.

Investigator John Grove, Monday, 10:40 AM

"415... 417... 419!"

John confirmed the address on his phone one last time. *419 Shady Elm Drive.*

Twenty seconds later he knocked on the front door.

Raised voices.

A male voice drew closer to the front door. John reached his right hand back and delicately placed it on his Beretta.

A man in his late forties answered the door, a little red in the face. "What?!!"

"Detective John Grove, Sacramento County Sheriff's," John flashed his badge with his left hand, keeping his right on his Beretta. "Are you Mr. Colton?"

The man paused for a moment, confused, then turned, totally ignoring John, and walked back toward the hallway shouting. "Did you already call the police?"

A female voice shouted from down the hall. "Not yet. But I should have! The little shit!"

The man shouted back. "He's your son!"

John stepped in the entryway.

The female voice grew louder. She appeared from the hallway and immediately got in her husband's face. "He's your son, too, at least the devious, coldhearted side of him!"

The man licked his lips and took a step toward her. "So am I to credit you with the passive aggressive, insane half?"

John stepped in between the two of them, "Enough!" The two cowered and took a step back, breathing heavy.

A dog sauntered into the room from the hallway. John recognized it as the dog from the pictures. John patted his leg, invitingly, and the dog trotted over to him tail wagging. He gave the dog a pet.

"Molly! Go lay down." Mr. Colton snapped.

The dog cowered, scurried to the kitchen and lay down in the corner.

"One question," John said, turning toward Mrs. Colton. "Why should have you called the cops?"

"Because our car went missing this morning."

"My Tahoe," Mr. Colton interjected. "And my keys are gone, so we know it's Brett... er... our son."

"How old is Brett?"

"He's fifteen," Mrs. Colton said. "A sophomore. But that wouldn't stop him from taking the car." She leaned toward John and raised her eyebrows. "He's been in trouble with the police before."

"Yeah," Mr. Colton pointed toward John. "Your guy had to come out and talk with him in January because he threatened some kids at school."

"Never did actually talk with him," Mrs. Colton corrected, turning toward her husband. "Brett wasn't here, and the officer never followed up."

"Tell me about these threats." John said.

"I don't really know. Just what the officer told us. Apparently, Brett posted something online about some kids he didn't like which resulted in some fight at school."

"Did you ever ask him about it?"

Both parents just looked at each other.

"He doesn't talk much." Mr. Colton said. "He just keeps to himself in his room with the door locked."

"Door locked?"

Both parents were quiet again.

"Can I please see his room?"

"Sure," Mr. Colton said, gesturing down the hallway. "Help yourself."

The three of them walked down the hallway and Mr. Colton tried to open the door. It was locked.

"A deadbolt?" John asked. "What fifteen-year-old has a dead-bolt?"

"His room is one of the only places he seems to *not* get into trouble." His dad argued. "I don't mind the deadbolt as long as he locks himself in there."

"Nice," John said. "Now do you have another key?"

Both parents shook their heads. "He bought the lock and in-stalled it himself."

John sighed.

"Permission to break in?" John asked.

His mom looked doubtful. "I don't know…"

"Well, do you want me to get your Tahoe back?"

"Yes!" Mr. Colton interjected. "Permission granted. I don't care if you break into the little bastard's room."

John couldn't help but notice the irony of the statement.

John backed up two steps and gave the door a front kick with the flat of his foot about six inches to the left of the deadbolt. The door jamb splintered like balsawood and the door swung open.

Mr. Colton flinched. "Holy shit! Don't you guys have a lock pick or something like that? I didn't mean destroy my house!"

John ignored them and walked into the middle of Brett's room. The parents hesitantly followed.

Mrs. Colton began picking up laundry lying around his bedroom.

"Don't!" John snapped.

She froze in her tracks.

"Just leave everything exactly how it is."

John stood in the middle of the room and slowly began scanning the room looking for… anything. The walls were covered with various band posters, mostly death metal: Autopsy, Vador, Carsass, My Chemical Romance…

"Who the hell names these bands?" John whispered to himself.

"Who the hell listens to this crap?" Mr. Colton scorned.

John turned to Mr. Colton. "Your son."

John squatted down and peered under the bed.

Nothing.

He lay down on his stomach and peered up under the mattresses.

"Aha!"

He stood up and flipped the mattresses up on end. There was a brown grocery bag shoved up inside the box spring. He pulled the bag out and dumped its contents onto the carpet in the middle of the room: a rifle cleaning kit, a few boxes of ammo, some electronic gadgets and a handful of fireworks.

John picked up one of the boxes of Ammo. *.223 Remington.* "Does your son own a gun?"

Mr. Colton laughed. "Of course not."

John picked up another box, this one of shotgun shells. Double-ought-buck. "He sure has a lot of ammo for someone without a weapon."

John exhaled and thought for a moment. "Do you have any idea where he acquired this stuff?" He didn't even know why he was asking them this question. He knew they didn't have a clue.

"I don't know," his mom answered, looking to her husband for any affirmation. "He's always buying and selling stuff on eBay. He's got like… a little business."

"Yeah . . . but didn't you notice him carrying weapons and ammo in and out of the house?"

"I wouldn't know because he always carries that big duffle bag with him."

"What duffle bag? Show me."

"It's his big green duffle bag. I think he keeps it in his closet right next to his laundry right over . . ." she pulled the left closet door open to see a large empty space.

Mrs. Colton scratched her head. "I guess he has it with him?"

John looked at Mrs. Colton. "Have you ever seen what's in that duffle bag?

She defensively backed up. "No. He said it was his baseball stuff."

"Does he play baseball?"

"Just with his friends after school."

"What friends?"

Mrs. Colton paused once again. Finally, she shook her head. "I don't know."

"Money. Does he have access to money, like this little eBay business?"

"No," Mrs. Colton shook her head. "Other than his college fund."

"College fund? Does he have access to that?"

Mrs. Colton shook her head confused. "Well, he's a co-signer, but he wouldn't touch that. His grandma left him that for college."

John sighed. "Do you have access to that account ma'am?"

"Uh... yes. I guess. I have an online sign in. I haven't used it in years, but I guess I could..."

"Please try."

"Let me go grab my laptop." Mrs. Colton left the room.

John stood up and glanced around the room, his eyes landing on the bookshelf. He walked over and reached behind each row of books, searching with his hands.

"What are you looking for?" Mr. Colton asked.

"What? Didn't you ever hide stuff behind your books when you were a kid?" John asked. "This was my favorite spot."

John's eyes lit up. He pulled out a small notebook from behind the second bookshelf.

John sat on the bed and began flipping through it. It appeared to be a journal of sorts. Drawings, quotes... journal entries.

Laugh at me. Go ahead. We'll see.

John flipped the page.

A single death is a tragedy; a million deaths is a statistic.
Joseph Stalin (1879—1953)

More drawings. He flipped through pages of drawings, landing on one that looked like a map. The word Cabrillo was scribbled at the top. The drawing wasn't very detailed. Someone that looked like a sniper was up on a hill. Kids were playing down in a park.

"Cabrillo?" John asked himself.

He flipped the page. More journal entries.

You think you're it. You think everyone loves you, but they only fear you. You're despised just like me. But yet you taunt.
Do it. Taunt. Point. I don't mind. Soon you'll see.
Wait until 420.

"420?"

"That's that pot-smoking code all the teenagers use," Mr. Colton said.

"Or it's a date," John said, more to himself than anyone else.

"Oh my God!" Mrs. Colton's voice shouted from the other room. "It's almost all gone!" She walked into the room staring at her laptop. "His grandma had left him $20,000 in this account."

"How much is left?" Mr. Colton roared.

Mrs. Colton looked up from the screen. "$3,427."

Mr. Colton threw up his hands. "Why did you let him have access to that account?!!"

"So it's my fault!"

Ignoring their banter, John set the journal aside and looked around the room again. A small garbage can was tucked under the computer desk.

John grabbed the garbage can and dumped its contents onto the floor. The Colton's stopped their bickering for a second to see what John was looking at. Gum wrappers. Wadded up paper and some pieces of torn up binder paper. John dropped to his knees and began sorting through the torn binder paper. The kid had obviously torn something up, but there were only about seven or eight pieces. *Obviously, this kid had never worked at the Pentagon.*

Within thirty seconds John had the pieces of paper constructed into its original form.

"Tape!" John demanded. "Scotch tape."

The two parents just stood there.

John reworded his request. "Do you have any tape, please?" John asked politely.

Mrs. Colton rolled her eyes and sighed. "Just a minute." She left the room.

A few minutes later John held the taped paper in his hands and began to digest the handwritten scribble.

And there it was again, dead center of the top of the page.

420

6:00	get up
6:10	load Tahoe—get out
Dead time—check gear	
10:40	arrive Cabrillo—set up decoy
10:48	set 15-minute delay
10:58ish	arrive at school
Gear up! (35 seconds)	
11:00	drop gear at perch—grab device
11:02	place device in Cafeteria—set timer
11:03	Park fun begins
11:04ish	Cabrillo 911 call. (4 to 8 minute response time in October.)
11:08	lunch bell

filler up!

11:17   *BOOM. Playtime! (9 minutes until first officer — 14 minutes before SWAT dispatched- 33 minutes until authorized to go in)*

John looked at his watch. "Oh no!"

911 Dispatch, Tuesday, 11:04 AM

Helen waved to Marlene as she returned to her desk. Only about twenty-five minutes to lunch, almost time for their little birthday celebration. Helen was turning 48 today, and Marlene was friend enough to remember. Nice someone remembered, Helen thought.

Helen's husband had left twelve years ago leaving her to finish raising her son. No other immediate family alive. But she had hopes of receiving at least a phone call from her son that night.

The phone rang. Back to work. She had grown to hate this job.

"911 — what is your emergency?"

Helen heard shots in the background and heavy breathing. A woman's voice finally screamed. "My son . . . I've got to get my son!"

"Where are you ma'am. Where is your son?" Helen didn't have a location because this was a cell phone. She needed to find out where.

The frantic voice answered, "He's over by the slide. I've got to get to him!"

"Ma'am. Where are you?"

"I'm at the park."

"Which park ma'am. I need your location if I'm going to help you."

"I don't know. It's the one on Manzanita and . . . wait . . . it's Fair Oaks . . . CABRILLO PARK! That's what it is. Cabrillo Park! Hurry. He's got a gun!"

"Hold on, ma'am." Helen moved quickly. She could hear shots being fired and that was enough. "All units, we have an ADW, shots fired at Cabrillo Park at Fair Oaks and Cabrillo. Unknown suspect. Unknown if any victims down at this time." Helen returned to the woman. "Who has the gun, ma'am? Your son?"

"No!" The woman screamed. "My son is two. He's by the . . ." the woman paused and then screamed. "Timothy get down! No Timothy. Lie down."

Helen heard movement again. Then she heard a child crying close to the phone, then the sound of the lady's voice crying and talking to the little boy, "It's okay, Timothy, it's okay."

"Ma'am. Are you both okay?"

There was a pause. Only breathing. "I think so." The sound of more shots fired, and the lady screamed. "Oh my God! He's trying to kill us."

"Who's trying to kill you, ma'am?" Helen urged.

Helen heard the woman crying hysterically. It sounded like she tried to talk but couldn't. Finally, she managed to speak. "I don't know. He's on the hill. I can see his gun."

"Ma'am. Is anyone hurt? Has anyone been shot?"

Again, a pause. Helen looked at Marlene who had finished her call and was now standing next to her. Phil, her supervisor was standing over her as well, talking to a police sergeant.

Helen heard the woman sniffing and then she answered. "I don't know. I don't think so."

"Where are you?"

"I'm by the playground. Behind a little cement thingy."

"Where is your son?" Helen didn't hear him crying anymore.

"He's right here." The woman let out a loud sigh that sounded like half a laugh. "He's playing with a dandelion. That's right, Timothy. It's a pretty flower."

Helen consoled the woman for a few minutes.

Phil whispered to Helen, "Officers were just around the corner. They should be arriving at the scene any second."

"Ma'am. Officers are arriving at the scene any second!"

Again, a pause. Then an emphatic, "Oh thank God! They just pulled up. Oh, my baby!" Then Helen heard shots. Then a scream, then baby crying. Then shots that sounded closer.

The line went dead.

Helen looked at Marlene.

Silence.

Investigator John Grove, Tuesday, 11:06 AM

John grabbed his radio and flicked on his lights and sirens. The Crown Vic peeled out.

He peeked at his watch: 11:06 a.m. He grabbed his radio.

"This is 1L19, I need all units to Mesa Rosa immediately. We have a potential school shooting going down right now!"

John looked to his left as he locked up his wheels into a power slide, hanging a hard right out of the neighborhood toward the school. The school was only two minutes away.

Dispatch came on the radio. "1L19, we can't spare any units for a *potential* shooting right now. All available units were just dispatched to an ADW in a park."

A park. What park? Then it hit him.

"Cabrillo Park?" John asked.

Silence.

Finally dispatch replied. "Affirmative. Cabrillo Park. All available units have just arrived on the scene."

John thought for a moment. It was actually going down just like it was written. Then he put the radio to his lips again, "Did they see a suspect yet?"

John power-slid around another corner onto San Juan. The school was just ahead.

Dispatch came on the radio again, "Negative. Unknown suspect. No visual yet."

John paused. *This white boy isn't stupid.*

"Dispatch. I need all available units to Mesa Rosa now," John said. "The ADW in the park is a hoax. I repeat. The ADW is a decoy. What's about to happen at Mesa is real!"

John waited for a response and slowed down as he approached Mesa's lower parking lot. He didn't know the school well. He had been there once or twice when he was younger for a baseball game, but that was it. It was one of the oldest schools in the Sacramento area. One of the few schools on the West Coast with a midwestern design.

Dispatch spoke again, "1L19. I relayed your message. They're sending you a unit."

"One unit?!!!" John screamed.

He threw the handset to the floorboard and spilled out a few of his favorite obscenities.

He kept his eyes peeled as he quickly moved his car through rows of cars to the front of the parking lot. He eyed a fire lane where he would leave his car. Right next to a handicapped spot with . . . a Navy-Blue Chevy Tahoe, parked crooked.

John stared at the SUV in the handicapped spot. *Blue Chevy Tahoe?*

John picked up the radio handset again. "Dispatch, this is 1L19 again. I need the fastest plate check you've ever run in your life. California tags, 1CXK302, I repeat, 1CXK302."

"Copy that," dispatch responded.

John popped out of his car and laid his hand on the hood of the Tahoe.

Warm.

He heard a bell in the distance. He could see students exiting one of the buildings and walking around the quad area with their lunches. He jumped back in the car and waited for dispatch.

Silence.

He tapped the radio's handset on the dashboard impatiently. Ten seconds passed, and John started to get out again when the radio cracked, "1L19. I've got that California plate for ya."

John picked up the radio's handset again. "Roger that—what is it?"

"1L19, license returns to a 2013 Chevy Tahoe, blue in color, RO information: Robert Colton, 419 Shady Oak Drive, Carmichael, California."

John's eyes grew big. "Dispatch. I've got a very pissed off kid with a shotgun, a rifle, and who knows what else at Mesa Rosa right now! And you've got a very convincing distraction over in Cabrillo Park. Tell those other units to forget the ADW in the park and get down here now!"

John threw the radio handset down, shoved his radio on his belt and checked the magazine on his 9MM for the second time that day.

He glanced at his watch: 11:12
He started running to a building marked Cafeteria.

Officer Paul Hubbard, Tuesday, 11:08 AM

As Paul Hubbard hung a left on Fair Oaks Blvd. half a block from Cabrillo Park, he could already hear shots being fired. Hubbard was the first to arrive on the scene. The shots seemed to be coming from a hill above the park. Two moms and what looked like five toddlers could be seen hiding, huddled behind various playground equipment.

He called in his position and quickly army crawled behind a cement partition, so he could get a better view of the sniper.

Being cautious to stay out of site, Hubbard attempted to peek through the bushes and catch sight of the suspect. The hill was about 100 yards away from his location, definitely too far to make anything out. But he unquestionably saw a gun barrel sticking out and what looked like a perp wearing a hat.

More shots rang out from the hilltops. Screams echoed throughout the playground.

Paul had a clear shot, so he returned fire toward the hill. *Nothing.*

The sniper kept shooting despite Paul's shots. No hesitation.

As a few more units pulled up, Paul noticed something peculiar. The report of the rifle sounded… *weird*. It actually didn't sound like a rifle at all. Maybe a shotgun… but not a rifle.

Who would use a shotgun from over 100 yards out? Was he shooting slugs?

Something else didn't make sense. It was hard to tell… but Paul definitely didn't see any muzzle flash coming from the gun. Not to mention, this guy must have been a terrible shot. Not a single round had come near anyone.

Paul had been in two shootouts in his career. In one of them, the assailant turned his gun toward the squad cars as soon as they pulled up. Didn't hit any cops, but made Swiss cheese of the doors of his Crown Vic.

This guy hadn't hit jack…

Three officers crawled up next to Paul. "What have we got?"

Paul turned around, sat and wiped his eyes with his forearms. "It just don't add up."

Brett, Tuesday, Tuesday, 11:11 AM

Brett laid flat on the roof of the track house. He'd only been up here one time before when he was scouting locations a few months ago. The view of the cafeteria was perfect.

Brett extended the legs of his rifle's bipod and looked through the scope. The main west doors going into the cafeteria were in clear view. Sixty yards, tops.

He looked at his watch and his heart started to beat even faster. It was 11:16 and 56 seconds, 57, 58, 59…

Investigator John Grove, Tuesday, 11:12 AM

John slowed down to a walk as he approached the cafeteria. He ducked off to the side by a ravine that ran alongside the cafeteria and the parking lot. He pulled the taped-up piece of paper from his pocket and scanned the handwritten schedule.

> 11:02   *place device in Cafeteria—*
> *check timer*

John looked at his watch again. 11:13.
Too late.
He skimmed down the sheet to the bottom.

> 11:08   *lunch bell*
>
> *filler up!*
>
> 11:17   *BOOM. Playtime! (9*
> *minutes until first officer –*
> *14 minutes before SWAT*
> *dispatched- 33 minutes*
> *until authorized to go in)*

John looked at his watch again and saw it click to 11:14.
Three minutes… *barely!*
He barged into the cafeteria. It was packed full of students. The students at the table near his doors stared at him, but he didn't waste any time, he began scanning the room for a big green duffle bag. The wall to his right had about fifty cubbies built into it and was full of backpacks and duffle bags, most of them pretty small. Only a few large duffle bags.
John ran over and started looking for a green one.
Red.
Red.
Black.

Red.

"Where the hell is a green duffle bag?" John muttered to himself.

A large *blue* duffle bag lay against the wall, surrounded by countless backpacks. It was by far larger than any other bag in the building.

"Green, my ass!" John mumbled and scampered towards the bag.

He unzipped it and peered inside.

His heart stopped midbeat.

He was staring at a homemade fertilizer bomb big enough to blow the roof off of the building. A timer was attached, and it was clicking down from fifty-six seconds.

John turned towards the teenagers... but second-guessed himself.

No time to evacuate hundreds.

He grabbed the bag, threw it over his shoulder and ran towards the doors he had entered, counting out loud to himself.

"48, 47, 46..."

Bursting out the doors he hung a right and headed toward the ravine.

"39, 38, 37..."

John scanned the ravine.

Clear.

He threw the bag to the bottom of the ravine and turned back towards the building in full sprint.

"26, 25, 24..."

John burst in the doors for the second time that day.

"Everyone down on the ground, now!" he shouted.

Hundreds of students just stared at him, not moving in the slightest.

John couldn't believe what he was seeing. *Morons!*

He pulled out his badge, drew his gun and began waving it in the air.

"I said down on the ground. Now!"

Students all dropped to the ground immediately.

John followed suit, hitting the ground and covered his ears. He had lost count, but he figured the device should have hit zero by now.

Seconds passed. Kids heads began to rise, staring at John with uncertain looks. Some even started to get up.

John yelled, "I said down. I'm not kidding. There is a…"

A deafening explosion shook the building and every window on the east entrance shattered, shooting glass throughout the entire east side of the cafeteria. Pieces of glass landed all around John.

Students began screaming and running towards the west entrance.

"No!" John screamed.

But no one was listening. Hundreds of students began pouring out the west entrance of the cafeteria facing the track.

Mrs. Allison, Tuesday, 11:17 AM

"So how could you make these two sentences better?"

Nancy habitually tapped her pen up and down between her teeth, waiting for a response.

"Come on. Think about it. You've got two simple sentences that could be combined. Is it possible we can take this one and make a dependent clause…"

A thunderous boom shook the building.

The students ran to the window to look out at lower campus. Nancy went to the window as well.

A large gray cloud expanded skyward from near the parking lot.

"Everyone stay put." Nancy commanded. "No one leaves this room."

Clint Havard, Tuesday, 11:17 AM

Clint climbed up to the second to last rung of the ladder, being careful not to drop the florescent bulb. The fluorescent lights in the Drake building were old and worked sporadically. Clint had put in a request to Mrs. Hippo last year to replace them all with LED or even T8 lighting. Brighter and four times the lifespan. Hippo never even bothered to respond.

Useless walrus.

As Clint reached up to rotate the long tube into place, an enormous roar shook the building, almost knocking him off balance atop of the eight-foot ladder.

"What the..."

He steadied himself from falling and quickly climbed down the ladder.

Walking over to the nearest window he saw a dark gray billowing cloud rising from near the cafeteria.

Clint sprinted down the hallway.

Michael, Wednesday, Tuesday, 11:17 AM

Where was Cordell?

Michael bobbed his head to the music… just a little. Nothing noticeable, but it was hard to resist Bruno's beats.

24K Magic
Bruno Mars

Funny, Cordell was usually in the student center by now, but Michael hadn't seen him yet. So he just hung with Deeby, enjoying the music.

Michael gave a quick head nod to Ashley, complimenting her for getting the place turnt. The girl always had good stuff playing. Always!

I'm a dangerous man with some money in my pocket…

Tyler, Blake and a few others walked in, but no…
Boom.
The room quaked.
Ashley turned the volume down and looked at Michael.
"What was that?"
"I don't know."
Students began running to the windows. "Holy…"
Michael walked over to the window suspiciously. No one could see clearly because of the trees, but smoke was coming from somewhere over by the parking lot.
The janitor sprinted past in the hallway.
A teacher poked his head out of one of the classes down the hall, then cautiously made his way into the hallway. When he saw the students in the student center, he told them to stay put.
Why do teachers always think they need to tell us to stay put?
Deeby and Michael sat down on the couch next to Tyler and Blake. Large Marge ran past heading toward the north hallway.
"That's no moon. It's a space station." Deeby quipped.

Tyler and Blake chuckled.

"Do you even know what you're laughing at?" Michael asked them.

"What?" Blake shrugged his shoulders. "I love Star Trek."

Chris and Luke appeared, saw the guys and walked over.

"What's going on?" Chris asked.

"Let's go find out," Luke said.

"I'm going to wait and see if I can find Cordell," Michael said.

"Suit yourself," Luke said, and set out with Chris, Tyler, Blake and Deeby in tow.

Michael went to the window again.

Where was Cordell?

Brett, Tuesday, Tuesday, 11:17 AM

The explosion echoed throughout the campus. Brett covered his eyes and buried his head for a few seconds. Then he looked up to see his handiwork.

Something was wrong. The building was completely intact. *The blast... it was too far away.*

He couldn't see any damage to the cafeteria.

Brett's whole body tensed up.

Students began pouring out of the west entrance.

"How could they have . . .?" Brett couldn't figure out what happened. But he wasn't going to miss out on his chance.

He pulled the scope of his AR15 to his right eye and aimed at the students coming out the west doors. Brett recognized so many faces.

His finger touched the trigger. It was time. This was the moment he had been waiting for.

He squeezed the trigger.

Investigator John Grove, Tuesday, 11:17 AM

John sprang up and began leaping across tables towards the west entrance of the cafeteria. Some students were huddling in groups across the floor, but most were rushing towards the exits.

"Stop! Stay inside!"

No one listened.

The report of a rifle rang out from the west side of the building. Then again, and again.

Distant screams.

Oh no...

John bounded across five more tables, almost slipping on the second to last one, but catching himself mid-stumble.

"Stop! Sniper outside!"

A haphazard group of students stopped. Others weren't processing anything, they were just in flight mode, and continued pouring out of the west doors.

A group of students parted the way for John as he sprang from the last table and headed for the door.

Two more shots rang out beyond the doors. Screams followed.

John threw his body up against the brick wall just inside the west doors, gun drawn.

More students emptied out the doors. John finally jumped in front of the two main doors, waving his gun.

"Stop! Go back!" John screamed, holding out his hand.

A small nervous freshman wearing a blue Jansport backpack and a Nike T-shirt darted out the doors to the right of John, swinging it wide open. John saw the boy get three yards then his body dropped to the ground like he had been punched by a freight train. A gunshot rang out before the boy's body hit the ground.

John recognized the rifle's report; at least it sounded a lot like an M16. He knew that sound well. Although it was just one shot. So it was probably an AR15, the "semi-auto" equivalent.

Students inside the cafeteria screamed and hit the ground.

John peeked outside as the door slowly closed automatically. He saw four bodies lying on the walkways just outside the doors.

Anyone walking out these doors was completely exposed. John knew this wasn't his exit. He began making his way back across the cafeteria toward the east entrance once again. He would try to find a way around.

He grabbed his portable radio. "Bomb at Mesa Rosa. Shots fired. I've got at least four students down, probably more. When can I have those units?"

John added a few more choice words to get the point across.

PART IV

"Death is nothing to us, since when we are,
death has not come,
and when death has come, we are not."

-Epicurus

Lieutenant Paul Hubbard, Tuesday, 11:18 AM

Paul watched as two officers began working their way around the perimeter of the park trying to flank the sniper.

His radio squawked.

"A bomb just detonated at Mesa Rosa. ADW. Shots fired. Multiple fatalities. All available units please respond."

Paul grabbed his radio and turned to the officer next to him. "What's going on today?"

He spoke into the radio. "This is 1L13. We've got several units engaged at this moment. We can't spare any units. We still got an unknown gunman here shooting at families."

"Look!" The officer next to him pointed up towards the sniper on the hill.

The two officers who had made their way around the hill were just standing next to the sniper. One officer had his hand on his hip.

Paul's radio squawked again. It was the officer standing up by the sniper. "1L13, we've got ourselves a decoy here."

Two minutes later Paul was up on the barricade staring at a dummy wearing a hat with a BB gun propped up and aimed at the playground below. A small technical device was on the ground next to an enormous string of what looked like M80s or maybe even quarter sticks of dynamite.

One of the officers who found the dummy asked, "What's this all about?"

Paul Hubbard didn't even answer. He just motioned everyone down the hill and lifted his radio to his mouth. "Dispatch, this is 1L13. We are on our way to Mesa Rosa now."

Brett, Tuesday, Tuesday, 11:18 AM

Four... no five.

Brett's heart raced as he ejected the magazine, flipped it and popped the other magazine in. A new magazine meant Brett had already spent thirty rounds. He had only hit six or seven students so far, and two of them got up again and kept running. Brett was flooded with emotion. Excitement... fear...disbelief. He couldn't shake the images of those students' bodies flailing when he hit his mark. He clenched his teeth. What happened to his bomb? Hundreds should be dead right now. Instead... what... *five?*

The flow of students out the west doors slowed to a trickle.

Brett retracted his bipod and slid across the roof, easily dropping to the ground on the west side of the track house, out of sight from the cafeteria. He reached into his bag and collected his shotgun and his alien mask. Slipping the mask over his head, he noticed once again how the bulging eyes provided great peripheral vision.

Part I of his plan hadn't worked out so good. No worries. *Part II couldn't fail.* He flung his AR15 over his shoulder, picked up his shotgun and checked his gear one last time. Everything was in place. He placed earbuds in his ears once again and carefully selected a song from his playlist.

> *Cannibal Corpse*
> Hammer Smashed Face

Brett cracked a smile as the music surged through his body.

There's something inside me. It's, it's coming out, I feel like killing you

No song could be more appropriate.

He picked up his bag and ran towards the Drake Building.

At one with my sixth sense, I feel free, to kill as I please, no one can stop me...

Mrs. Allison, Tuesday, 11:20 AM

Nancy poked her head out of her classroom. Shane Dulvers, a biology teacher, was walking down the hall towards the student center.

Dan poked his head out of his classroom across the hall.

"What was that?"

"Something exploded down by the parking lot, followed by gunshots."

"Gunshots? Are you sure?"

Nancy asked herself the same question. *Are you sure you heard gunshots, Sergeant Allison?*

Other than basic and at the range, Nancy had only heard live gunshots one other time, a memorable night as an MP.

"Yes," Nancy said. "I'm sure."

"Should we evacuate the kids?" Dan asked.

"I don't think so," Nancy answered. "Who knows what's down there."

"Good point," Dan paused. "So what now?"

"Let's wait it out a few more minutes and see what admin wants us to do," she replied.

"Agreed," Dan ducked his head back in his room and said something to his class.

Nancy shut her door and went to the window again to try to get a better look. She pressed against the window and peered at an awkward angle toward the South entrance of the building. She saw a few students running up the hill.

She returned her gaze to her classroom. Most the students in her class were looking at their phones.

She pulled out her phone. It still worked, despite the cracked screen. She dialed the front office. It rang seven times.

No answer.

She set her phone on the windowsill and tried to open one of the windows to see if she could hear what was happening outside.

"Mrs. Allison. Can we go down there and see what's going on?" a student named Lindsey asked.

"Let's hold up a few minutes. I want to see…"

Thunderous shots rang out somewhere in the hallway.

Time stopped.

The earsplitting weapon fire was only augmented by the deathly silence that followed. Nancy's students looked to her for comfort… for hope, but her face gave her away. Fear enveloped the room like the ominous hush.

But the silence was fleeting.

Screams.

Sounded like downstairs. Maybe directly below them.

Nancy ran to the door again and peeked her head out into the hallway. Screams echoed the hallways below and up the south stairwell.

Voices.

"He's got a gun!"

Brett, Tuesday, 11:24 AM

Brett burst into the south doors of the Drake building. Random students wandered the hallways, many of them gathering by the Lobby's side windows trying to catch a glimpse of whatever it was that caused the smoke and the noise outside. One student was taking video of the smoke with his phone.

A couple students turned to see the masked figure standing in the doorway.

Brett pointed his shotgun in the direction of a junior wearing a football jersey. He pulled the trigger of the weapon for the first time since in the woods a month before. The young athlete's body fell back and dropped to the ground like someone snipped the strings above a marionette.

The blast was deafening in the reverberating hallway, even with his earbuds in.

A surprising silence blanketed the room for what seemed like seconds as the other students processed the horror they had just seen unfold before their eyes.

And cue.

Screams echoed through the hallway.

Brett pointed the gun at the three students nearest to him as they fled. He pulled the trigger twice.

Blam. Blam.

Two more fell, and another stumbled.

Brett turned around and pulled a roll of duct tape out of his bag along with another device, no bigger than a shoebox. He disconnected the device into two pieces and taped each half of the device to the double doors. He carefully connected two wires together from one device to the next and then flicked a switch. A little red light turned on.

One down; two to go.

Heads poked out of random classrooms like vertical prairie dogs as he finished arming his device. Brett swung his 12-gauge toward a teacher to his right, about twenty feet out. The teacher ducked his head back in just in time as Brett fired at the door. As the blast resonated down the corridor, the other teachers withdrew their heads as well, locking their doors and fleeing to the back of their rooms.

Brett approached the door he had just filled with double-ought. He reached for the knob... it turned.

Didn't even lock the door?

A cluster of twenty-plus students huddled in the corner behind the teacher. Seniors mostly. Half of them were crying as they talked into their phones. Several started wailing when they saw the masked gunman.

"Please," the teacher begged. "Please don't!"

"Funny," the alien said. "That's exactly what I always said."

Kari, Tuesday 11:26 AM

Shots echoed through the hallway. Kids ran by screaming. "He's got a gun!"

"Who?" Kari shouted, grabbing her backpack off the table.

No one stopped to answer. They just scurried toward the north stairwell.

Kari poked her head out of the library. She didn't see anything down the hall, but she could only see as far as the student center.

Shots resounded from downstairs, echoing up the stairwell.

More screams.

"They're coming!"

Kari ran away from the stairwell. As she approached the student center, a crowd of students ran toward her screaming. Kari stopped and pressed herself against the wall, confused about where to go.

Students ran by. One boy was talking on his phone while he ran. "There are bodies on the ground! He's shooting everyone!"

Kari heard screams coming from both directions in the hallway. Students passed her coming from the north stairwell. She saw students disappear into a classroom down the hallway and lock the door behind them.

The corridor emptied.

She looked across the hallway and saw a door labeled Maintenance Closet.

More shots from downstairs.

Screams.

"Forget this!"

Cordell, Tuesday, 11:24 AM

"Are you going to the parking lot to check it out?" Jake asked.

"Yeah. As soon as we find Michael," Nick said. "I think he's up in the student center."

Cordell and Nick ran up the south stairwell toward the student center where they typically connected with Michael during lunch. When they reached the top of the stairs they heard an ear-splitting boom.

Cordell and Nick ducked and looked at each other.

Screams.

Two more blasts echoed up the stairway followed by more screams.

Cordell slowly crept down the stairs and peeked around the corner. Nick followed.

Jake's body was sprawled out in the hallway below in a twisted heap. Two more bodies lay behind him, both of them Jake's friends, one named Haley. Cordell didn't know the other's name.

They heard movement near the outside doors, just out of sight from where they stood in the stairwell.

Cordell turned to whisper to Nick, then another blast shook the stairway.

Cordell whipped around to see a masked figure walking down the hall away from the stairwell toward a classroom.

He didn't see us!

The lanky masked teenager turned the doorknob and entered the classroom, stepping out of sight.

Crying.

Voices.

Blasts echoed out of the classroom.

Cordell and Nick ran upstairs.

More shots, but a different sound. Pops, instead of booms.

The first door on their right was Cordell's sophomore English class. He tried the doorknob. It was locked. They tried two more doors. *Locked. Locked.*

The fourth door on the right was open. The two burst inside.

Empty.

They locked the door behind them and ran toward the windows. Cordell looked out the windows. Way too high to jump.

"What now?" Nick asked.

Cordell turned and looked around the classroom. "We just lay low and play it cool."

The two sat down on the floor in the corner of the room behind the teacher's desk.

Nick pulled out his phone and started dialing 911. "Who do you think that is?" he asked Cordell while pressing the green button to dial.

"Seriously?" Cordell raised his eyebrows. "You don't know?"

Nick lowered his phone. "You mean... *you do?*"

Investigator John Grove, Tuesday, 11:20 AM

By the time John skirted his way around the cafeteria to a position where he could possibly engage against the sniper, the shooting had stopped.

John cautiously scouted where the shots might have come from in case the sniper was still there waiting it out. An old shed had a perfect view of the cafeteria's west entrance.

As John crawled up toward the shed he heard shots from the big building on the top of the hill across campus.

John started toward the building but noticed three students huddled around an injured teen lying on the sidewalk. When they saw John, they pleaded for his help. The student had been shot in the shoulder and was lying in a pool of his own blood.

He looked up at the building, then back to the injured teen.

John ran over to the teen to assess his condition. The kid was grossly pale and blood was seeping out of his wound.

John looked up at one of the guys in the group. "Give me your sweatshirt." The young teenager quickly took off his sweatshirt and handed it to John. John pressed it against the injured teen's shoulder with his left hand. The boy let out a loud wail.

John looked up at the cluster of students huddled together — a cheerleader and two guys.

"Is he going to be all right?" The cheerleader asked.

"Yes," John affirmed optimistically. "What's your name?"

"Megan."

"Were you here when it happened, Megan?"

"He was running right behind me; next thing I knew he was on the ground. He got back up, so I helped him duck out of sight."

"You did good Megan," John grabbed Megan's hands and placed them on the sweatshirt. "Now keep pressure on this until the ambulance arrives."

John looked down and saw blood on his hands. It was from Megan's arm.

"Megan. You're bleeding."

"It's just a scrape." Megan responded, keeping pressure on the other student's wound.

John gently moved Megan's sleeve and looked at the wound. "This isn't a scrape. You've been shot." John peeked his head around her arm and investigated. "It barely hit your forearm, but it tore up your muscle. Let me wrap something around it."

"I'm fine." Megan said. "He's worse. Just get him help."

John ignored Megan and looked at one of the other guys. "Give me your t-shirt. Now."

The student quickly took off his t-shirt. John tore it into strips and wrapped one of the strips around Megan's arm while she kept pressure on the other student's wound."

John looked at Megan. "Are you good?"

Megan nodded. "I got this."

"Unbelievable." John said, shaking his head. "You're a rarity among cheerleaders, Megan!"

John stood and looked around the campus as he grabbed his radio. "Control, this is John Grove still out at Mesa Rosa. I've got at least five dead and three injured. If I don't get an ambulance here soon we're going to lose another one. Please."

John tucked his radio back in his belt and turned toward the three teens. "Help will be here soon, but the ambulance won't come up here with a shooter. So I need you three to pick him up, gently carry him down to the curb by the parking lot and stay there until the ambulance arrives. Got it?"

Megan got up and reached down to pick the injured boy up. The other two just stared.

"Well come on!" Megan shouted. "I can't lift him by myself! Grab his feet."

The other two got up and each grabbed a leg.

A minute later John was up against the wall near the south entrance of the Drake building. He quickly peeked through the glass doors.

Nothing.

He peeked slowly again, this time getting a better glimpse down the hallway. Three bodies lay on the floor not ten feet from the door.

Shots bellowed from somewhere deep inside the building. John reached for the door... then froze when he saw a blinking red light.

The doors had a device installed near the push bar of each door.

John cursed to himself and then pulled out his radio once again. "Control, I need bomb squad. I'm staring at yet another device attached to the entrance of this building at Mesa Rosa, and if it's anything like the last one..." John didn't bother finishing the sentence. "The building is..." John backed up and noted the sign over the door. "It's the Drake building. Shots fired. I'm going to try to find another way in."

John hugged the perimeter of the building and worked around the other side. As he did, he heard more shots from inside.

His radio squawked.

"1L19, this is Control. We're receiving numerous calls from students and teachers at Mesa Rosa. There are students hiding all over campus, apparently hundreds..."

John's phone started vibrating. He glanced at the number. It was from his boss.

"Thanks Control." John interrupted. "I've got Lieutenant Ferris on the other line. 1L19 out."

John pressed the green button on his phone. "This is Grove."

"Detective Grove. This is Lieutenant Ferris. I've been in the loop this whole time. I want you to wait outside until bomb squad arrives. Copy?"

John scowled. "Lieutenant Ferris. I copy that, but I just heard more shots from inside. If I can find another entrance, I'm going in."

"Detective Grove. We've already had one bomb detonate on this campus today, correct?"

"Yes," John replied. "But if I don't engage now..."

"Grove. Do you want to accidentally detonate a bomb and kill hundreds of kids because you couldn't wait a couple of minutes until bomb squad arrives? You will hold your position. That is an order."

John hit END and let out a few more obscenities.

Michael, Tuesday, 11:26 AM

Students ran through the student center screaming. "He's shooting everyone!"

"Who?" Michael asked, trying to get a girl's attention as she ran past.

"Someone in a mask. He just killed Jake," She began bawling and ran toward the north stairwell.

Shots rang out from the floor below. It was hard to decipher from where. It sounded like it was closer to the south stairwell. So Michael headed the opposite way, passing students running both ways.

More shots, seconds apart. Then even more from a different gun.

A crowd of students dispensed from the north stairwell. Many of them stopped trying random doors. Not a bad idea, but most doors were locked.

Michael tried a door to the right. It was locked. He looked through the small window and saw movement. Students were barricading the door with desks.

Michael knocked quietly and whispered. "Hey! Let me in."

He tried the doorknob again.

He could hear voices on the other side of the door. "Don't let him in. It could be one of them."

Large Marge came running up the stairway, breathing heavily. "Lock the doors. They are going classroom to classroom." She began trying random doors as well. When one didn't open she pulled out a set of keys from her pocket and began looking for the right key.

Shots resounded up the north stairwell.

Marge jumped at the sound, dropping her keys, and ran past Michael panic-stricken.

Michael grabbed her keys and tried a nearby door. It was a teacher's lounge. He had seen Mr. Travers and Mrs. Shultz go in here each day during lunch.

More shots.

The third key he tried unlocked the door.

Michael walked in and took a quick inventory of the room. Three teachers huddled in the corner.

"What are you doing in here! Get out!"

It was his old History teacher Mr. Shaw. *Of all people.*

"Can't do that." Michael said. "There's crazy people with guns downstairs!"

"Well, shut the door, quickly!" another teacher shouted. Michael didn't know who she was. Had seen her around campus.

He locked the door behind him and walked through to the other door that opened directly into a classroom. It was unlocked.

The classroom was completely silent. The teacher's desk was pushed against the hallway door and a file cabinet was laid down on top of it.

Michael heard a whisper across the classroom.

He walked over to the other side of the room and saw about a dozen kids crouched down behind a small bookshelf. Ryan Ratner was there, Matt Bentley… *and Sierra!*

Another girl in a red sweater started cowering when she saw Michael. "Don't hurt us! Don't hurt us!"

"Relax," Michael said, putting out his hand. "You're safe. They're downstairs still, and the doors are locked."

Another girl in the group was on the phone describing what happened to someone.

"911," Ryan said. "She's been on the phone with them for a couple of minutes."

"How'd you get in?" a cheerleader asked—a friend of Taylor Withers. Michael had seen her around campus but didn't know her name.

Michael didn't answer. I just held up the keys and jingled them.

He turned to Sierra. "You okay?"

She shrugged her shoulders and wiped a tear. "I… I don't know."

A shot resounded in the hallway. It sounded louder. Maybe upstairs. The girl in the red sweater started breathing heavy again.

"We've got to find us a way out of this building," Michael said, looking over to Ryan and Matt.

"Why?" Ryan snapped. "Let's just stay here!"

"Because if I got in here this easy, who says they can't too?"

Their faces revealed they agreed.

Another shot.

"Let's get out of here before this gets worse," Michael said, looking at the group. "So who's with me?"

The girls looked to the guys.

"I'm staying put!" Ryan said.

Michael looked at Matt. He just put his head down, ignoring everyone's stares. He didn't have to say a word. Michael knew his answer.

Michael sighed. "I'll go out through the teacher's lounge and lock the door behind me." He looked at Sierra. "You'll be safe for now. I'm just going to scout it out. I'll be back."

I'll be back. Of course, Deeby isn't here to hear me saying that line.

A minute later Michael was in the hallway. No sign of anyone. The empty corridor was completely deserted. An eerie feeling crept over Michael as he wandered through the post-apocalyptic scene. Scattered books dropped mid-flight. A random red binder laying open. A tattered blue backpack abandoned in the middle of the hallway.

He headed toward the student center quietly.

A shot rang out somewhere down the hall, around the corner in front of him.

More screams.

He turned around and sprinted back toward the north stairwell, then froze in his tracks.

What if the other one was waiting downstairs for me?

He thought for a moment.

How many were there?

He heard footsteps in the distance from the stairwell in front of him.

It was too late to turn back toward the teachers' lounge. He pulled out Large Marge's keys and tried the door to his right, using the same key as the teachers' lounge. It opened first try.

He slipped in quietly and locked the doors behind him. It was some type of maintenance room.

He heard breathing behind him.

Spinning around, he saw Church Girl hiding behind a big air unit.

"You!"

It probably sounded a little harsher than he meant it, but let's just say Kari was one of the last people he wanted to spend any time with, especially locked in a closet.

A blast rang out from down the hallway.

"Don't hurt me! Please don't hurt me!" she begged.

Michael turned to her confused. "Why would I…" And then it dawned on him. "Oh. No. I'm not one of them…"

Another shot rang out. It sounded like it was down the hall.

"How do I know you're not one of them?" she demanded.

"Shhhhh!" he motioned for her to be quiet. He pressed his ear to the door, then leaned toward her and whispered,

"Listen Church Girl, if someone is going around shooting in these hallways, it ain't a brotha. Trust me. You know that's gotta be some crazy white-boy shit. Have you ever heard of a black school shooter?"

Her eyes looked down—like he was actually getting through to her.

Ignoring her, he looked around the closet trying to figure out if this was a wise place to be, especially considering present company.

She glared at Michael again. "Church Girl?!"

Michael sighed. *Maybe this room wasn't such a good idea.* He reached his hand toward the doorknob and three deafening shots rang out in the hallway somewhere close outside the door.

The two of them froze.

Scattered screams echoed through the hallways. Then silence.

The horror of what was happening crept in with the stillness. Death was paying the school a visit, and for all Michael and Kari knew, they were next. And that was part of what was so terrifying: they *didn't* know. The two of them had no idea what lurked in the halls. Michael hadn't seen a thing, and apparently neither had Kari.

More shots.

Michael was no gun expert, but he knew this. That was a big gun.

Kari started breathing louder and faster. She closed her eyes for a second. "Please God, please God ..."

"Shhhh!" Michael gave her a harsh look and put his finger to his lips.

The silence continued outside the door. Occasionally, faint screams could be heard from far away.

Michael quietly tried to glance around the room, scanning for hiding places. There was nowhere to hide in this stupid closet.

Why did I leave Sierra?

The closet was smaller than his apartment's kitchen. His gaze returned to the big steel door he had just come through.

Hinges.

That was good. "This door opens inward." Michael whispered. "We can barricade it."

He scanned the room for anything heavy. Boxes were stacked in one corner of the room. One of them was open. He looked in the box. Some kind of floor tiles. He tried to lift the box. Heavy. They would work.

He started stacking the heavy boxes against the door as quietly as he could. Kari looked at him confused.

"What are you doing?" she finally asked, still in the corner looking paranoid.

"Same thing everyone else is doing. Hiding and barricading from..." he stopped stacking boxes for a second. "Did you see who it was?"

"No," she said. "I just heard shots, and this was the first door I saw."

"At least you locked it." he mumbled, stacking another box by the door.

Kari looked confused. "Wait... how did you..."

Michael sighed, reached into his pocket and showed her the keys.

"Where did you get those?"

"Large Marge. She fled and left her keys."

Shots echoed in the hallway. They sounded distant, maybe downstairs.

Silence.

Kari began helping Michael barricade the door. They stacked two piles pretty high, using all but five boxes.

Michael backed away from the door, scanning the room again, taking mental inventory. Finally, he exhaled and leaned against one of the sidewalls to catch his breath.

Kari looked at the barricade they had constructed. Her gaze drifted to the five other boxes, then back to the door again. She paused; then she began adding the other five boxes.

Mrs. Allison, Tuesday, 11:29

"Lock your doors, they're coming!"

Students rushed by Nancy's room toward the south stairwell. Others fled the opposite way.

Nancy had heard a shot from downstairs moments before, so she poked her head out the door again. More students ran by. Dan poked his head out of his classroom.

Numerous blasts resounded from downstairs. The most she had heard yet. Screams.

A group of students emerged from the south stairwell. A sobbing girl who couldn't have been older than a freshman screamed as she passed Nancy, "He's going into the classrooms and shooting everyone!"

Other students yelled. "Barricade the doors."

"Bring your kids over here," Dan said. "I'm going to barricade this door."

Shots rang from the stairwell.

"No time!" Nancy closed the door and locked it.

"Help me with this," she called out to two of her students sitting within an arm's reach. "Let's slide this in front of the door."

The two boys pocketed their phones and the three of them slid a large bookcase in front of the door. Then they wedged her desk in front of the bookcase. The old desk's legs made a terrible screech as it dragged along the floor.

No sooner was the desk in place when the doorknob wiggled. Everyone froze.

The room was deathly still, save for the nagging second hand of the clock that taunted like some kind of countdown.

A gun blast exploded through their door, sending books flying from the bookshelf. The sound was earsplitting. The student's ears were momentarily deafened followed by a distinct ringing.

The students screamed and scrambled toward the back wall of the classroom. A second blast shot through the door, louder than the first. And this time, the bookshelf started to move.

Someone was pushing the door from the other side. The legs of the desk squeaked as it moved an inch.

The students screamed again, pressing up against the wall and covering their ears.

Someone pounded on the front door again and the desk budged another inch. The barricade wasn't holding.

Completely across the room, the door to the teachers' lounge swung open.

Clint the janitor poked his head into the room as the hallway door was still being pounded by the unknown gunman.

"Come with me. Quickly!" Clint whispered, and motioned with his hands.

Nancy looked at her students and they all looked to her for direction.

The desk squeaked again as the hallway door shifted another inch.

"Let's go!" Nancy announced, and all twenty-seven students scrambled towards the teachers' lounge.

Nancy swiped up her purse as she passed her chair, following the last student into the teachers' lounge. Clint held the door until she was through then quickly closed it behind her. He locked it and then immediately threw his shoulder into the refrigerator knocking it to the ground with a thud. He looked at Nancy. "Come on soldier," and gripped the fridge. Nancy grabbed it too and the two of them slid it in front of the door.

"That should slow him down at least."

He led them into the connecting classroom, which was already barricaded.

They heard another blast from the hallway outside of Nancy's classroom.

Clint removed a few coat hangers from the nearby shelving, threw them to the ground, removed the wooden dowel and laid it across his lap. He whipped out a six-inch buck knife and began carving the end to a nice point.

He looked up at Nancy mid stroke, "So where did you serve?"

Nancy cocked her head. "How did you know…"

He smiled.

Nancy raised her chin. "First Battalion, 505th Infantry, 82nd Airborne Division, Fort Bragg, North Carolina." She raised her eyebrows. "You?"

"BLT 1/8, Second Marine Division, Camp Lejeune, North Carolina."

"Thanks for saving our asses, Marine!" She opened her purse, pulled out her Smith & Wesson 380, chambered a round, flicked the safety off and aimed it at the door they had just entered.

Clint smiled for the second time that day. "Oorah!"

Sierra, Tuesday, 11:29 AM

Sierra looked at her phone again. Her mom hadn't replied to her calls or texts. Probably in the middle of her shift at work. That meant it could be hours before Sierra received a reply.

It had been quite a while since Michael left. Could those shots in the hallways have been shooting at him?

She punched in the passcode to her phone again, opened Snapchat and pinched the screen. Zooming in, she tried to find Michael. His bitmoji wasn't on the map. *Is your phone off?*

She pulled up her texts to Michael and typed a quick message to him.

Sierra: Are you OK?

She stared at the phone, hoping for a reply. Seconds turned to minutes.

Nothing.

She tried her friend Nicole.

Sierra: Where are you?

Ten seconds later her phone vibrated.

Nicky: Hiding in my bio lab. U OK???

Sierra sighed a breath of relief.

Sierra: I guess. We're hiding in Mrs. London's class. Do you know who's shooting?

Nicky: No. He's wearing a mask. He shot Jake, Haley and Kristi Directo. Angelica got shot in her side too and ran away. She's laying down here next to me. Mr. Ramsey is helping her. She's hurt really bad.

The girl to Sierra's right finished talking with 911.

"They're coming. They say the police are already here but stay put until they come get us from the classrooms."

The two guys gave high-fives to each other. "Yeah!"

Taylor Withers hugged her friend. "See, it's all..."

Another shot thundered in the hallway.

Everyone froze.

The girl next to Taylor began crying. She covered her mouth, trying to not make a sound.

Sierra: Did you hear that?

Nicky: Yeah. Sounded upstairs. Do you think he can get in?

Sierra: We barricaded our door with some really heavy stuff. Did you see him?

Nicky: Us too. Didn't see him. Angelica did. Said he's wearing a monster mask. But she's starting to say some pretty weird stuff.

Sierra: Wow.

Nicky: She looks really pale. I think she's seriously dying. I'm so freaked out. The police told us the paramedics can't come in yet. The shooter is still out there.

Sierra heard more screams in the hallway.

Sierra: Don't worry. Your door is barricaded. You're safe.

Nicky: She just coughed up blood. GTG

Sierra: I love you. Keep safe.

No more texts came through.

Sierra looked at the barricade they had constructed.

Was it safe?

She thought about what Nicky had written.

Monster mask.

Creepy.

She pulled out her phone and tried Michael again.

Sierra: Michael. Where R U?

Brett, Tuesday, 11:29 AM

Brett covertly moved through the hallways checking doorknobs as he went. By the time he had emerged from that first classroom, the hallways were a ghost town and most of the doors locked. He used the opportunity to reload his weapons—and set his two other devices.

Wandering back to the center of the main hallway, he paused at the vantage point and looked both ways waiting for anyone.

Nothing.

Slowly, he crept toward the north stairwell. The squeak of his shoes on the cheap floor echoed off the bare walls. The silence was unnerving. He turned to the right and shot a men's bathroom door to break the silence.

Screams seeped from various doors throughout the building. He peeked in the bathroom. No one was there.

The sound of approaching footsteps echoed down the stairwell. Two seniors rounded the corner, saw Brett, and froze in their tracks. Brett's 12-gauge opened fire. Both boys fell.

How many was that?

Three girls darted out of the ladies' bathroom about twenty yards behind him, rushing towards the south stairwell. Brett laughed.

He turned his weapon toward them and shot. They were a good fifty yards by the time he pulled the trigger. One of the girls buckled but kept running. They were quickly disappearing out of range. Brett started to switch to his AR15 but hesitated as the girls ascended up the south stairwell out of sight. He headed toward that stairwell. Soon Brett glided up the south stairway and navigated through the second-floor hallway.

He tried a door. His freshman science class.

Locked.

He moved down the hallway to the next door. His freshman English class. Mrs. Allison. He heard movement inside. Something being dragged across the floor. He tried the door.

Also locked.

He stood back from the door and shot the doorknob. The blast took out a huge chunk of the door. But it didn't seem to budge. Brett peered through one of the openings the blast had created. Something was wedged against the door.

Brett backed up and shot again. This time the blast completely took off the doorknob. Brett pushed on the door and it didn't budge. Whatever it was that was barricaded against it was heavy. He pushed again. It budged about an inch. Brett leaned in with all his weight... which wasn't much. The door slowly started to open, an inch at a time, if he was lucky.

Brett heard movement down the hallway. He stopped pushing for a moment to listen. He pulled out his earbuds to hear better.

Silence.

Brett pushed on the door some more until finally he had enough of an opening to peek through. He started to look through, but hesitated. What if someone was there waiting for him on the other side? He poked his barrel through and shot inside the classroom.

Silence.

He poked his head in and out of the classroom quickly. Nothing.

Forget this. There are other classrooms.

Mrs. Allison, Tuesday, 11:37 AM

Nancy held her aim at the door for at least ten minutes while Clint called 911.

Clint finished the call and hung up. "They're getting hundreds of calls, mostly students. I gave them a few more details about..."

Gunfire popped from down the hallway — a handgun.

She tilted her head. "That's a different gun."

She lowered her weapon. And flicked the safety.

"Yep. Pistol," Clint said.

"You think there's two gunmen?"

Clint shrugged his shoulders. "Not sure. Earlier I heard two weapons from downstairs. Seven shots from a shotgun, then about a dozen more from a pistol, probably in twenty seconds time."

"Could have been two gunmen, right?" Nancy asked. "You said you heard seven shotgun blasts. My Remington 870 holds four." Nancy said, thinking out loud. "But an extended magazine can hold up to six, plus one in the chamber."

"So what do you gotta do when your shotgun's empty?" Clint asked.

Nancy thought for a moment. "Either reload..."

"And if you don't have time?" Clint asked.

"Then you pull out a second weapon."

"And a Beretta can hold fifteen or even thirty in the magazine, a Glock holds seventeen..."

"So maybe it's one gunman."

"Could be. Don't get me wrong," Clint said, walking over to the window. "I'm not saying put your gun away."

Lindsey asked Nancy if there was any Kleenex. Nancy found a box on the desk and tossed it over to Lindsey, still carrying the gun in her right hand.

"Do you think we're safe, Mrs. Allison?" Lindsey asked, sniffling.

"We've got the room all barricaded, we've got a Marine in here, we've got weapons... I think we're safe in here for now," Nancy said, turning to Clint. "Right?"

Clint turned from the window. "For now."

"Are you allowed to have a gun at school?" Lindsey asked.

"Nope," Nancy said matter-of-factly.

Bennett, one of Nancy's freshman students, smiled really big. "I knew you were a bad girl!"

Nancy sighed. "You've really got to stop watching so much late-night Cinemax, Bennett."

She picked up her purse and looked for her phone.

It was gone.

Where...?

She reflected back to when she last used it.

I called the administration... no answer...then...

She cursed as she remembered. She set it by the windowsill.

"What?" Clint asked.

"My phone. It's in the other classroom."

"You can use mine," Clint said politely, and handed her his phone.

Nancy dialed Derek's number. It rang five times then went to voice mail.

She punched the red button, frustrated.

"No luck?" Clint asked.

"I tried my husband, but he probably didn't recognize the number. He hates all those spam calls."

Clint nodded. "I know, right?"

Nancy walked over to a space against the wall and sat down.

Clint sat down and leaned against a desk. He looked at Nancy's gun. "Is that a .38?"

"It's actually a .380. The .38 felt too small in my hands," Nancy locked the slide to the rear, ejecting the bullet into her hand, then reached over to him and handed him the gun. "It's the Smith & Wesson BODYGUARD® 380 with laser sighting. Best piece of personal protection a lady can carry these days." She turned towards the students. "And yes, I've got a permit for it!"

"How long did you serve?" Nancy asked as Clint examined her gun.

"Just two years. Medical discharge." Clint popped the magazine back in the small weapon.

"What happened?"

"Jihad happened," Clint said. He secured his grip around the handle activating the laser sight, aiming at the map on the wall. The red dot landed directly in the Middle East.

"Iran?" Nancy asked.

"Lebanon."

"Wait. When was this?"

Clint lowered the weapon, locked the slide to the rear and handed the gun back to Nancy.

"October 23, 1983."

Nancy's eyes grew big. "The Beirut barracks bombing? I thought I recognized your battalion name. I couldn't place it. You were there?"

Clint looked down at his shoes.

Nancy shook her head. "I'm sorry. I didn't mean to bring it up."

"What happened?" Bennett asked.

Clint looked up at the teen but didn't answer.

Luke, Tuesday, 11:37 AM

Luke tried another doorknob.

Locked.

"What the hell!" Luke yelled.

The five of them had been to almost every corner of the Drake building. At first, they ran downstairs until they heard shooting, so they turned back up the north stairway and ran through the upstairs hallways. It was there they heard yelling about the shooters, students running all different directions and barricading themselves in classrooms.

When more shots echoed from downstairs, Luke headed to the south end of the building. But once again, students ran past them from the south stairwell shouting, "He's coming!" So they turned back toward the north stairwell, trying every door they passed. Since all the doors seemed to be locked at this point, Luke ducked in one of the guys' bathrooms. The other four guys followed.

"This isn't a good idea," Deeby said.

"What?" Luke asked.

"We're hiding in a room with no other exits?" Deeby said. "How is this smart?"

"Because the door was open!" Luke snarled.

Deeby shook his head. "Nope. This is the scene in the movie where the audience starts yelling at the screen, 'You fools! Don't go in there!'"

"So where should we go?" Blake asked Deeby.

"Somewhere where we aren't pinned down," Deeby said.

"We stay," Luke barked.

Everyone looked at each other.

Finally, Deeby spoke up: "Sorry guys. I'm outta here."

Deeby headed for the door. Tyler, Chris and Blake looked at one another.

"Wait," Blake called to Deeby. Then he turned to Luke. "I think Deeby's got a point. I'm gonna roll with him."

Luke was silent for a moment. Then he shook his head. "Whatever, man."

Blake looked to Tyler and Chris. They both shrugged their shoulders and sat down.

Deeby and Blake peeked out into the hallway, then disappeared.

Luke locked the door and turned to Tyler and Chris. "I'm not roaming the halls and getting shot like those two dumbasses!"

Investigator John Grove, Tuesday, 11:46

John had checked the only three entrances to the building. All three had devices.

The sound of sirens approached. Even more units.

About time.

John grabbed his radio.

"Control, this is 1L19. I'm on site at Mesa Rosa and units are arriving. Have all units stand by so I can address them."

John paused for a moment.

"Attention all units arriving at Mesa Rosa, this is 1L19, Detective John Grove. Active shooter at the school, suspect is possibly and most likely Brett Colton, white, male, 5'10', blonde, 130 pounds, armed with shotgun and rifle..."

John sighed. "A bomb detonated on lower campus near the cafeteria, a sniper — most likely Colton — took out at least eight students, probably more, and now he is on foot in the big red building labeled Drake on upper campus. I have checked the perimeter and there are three entrances and all three have some sort of bomb rigged to the doors. I have heard shots fired as recently as three minutes ago. The shooter is still at large, and we've got hundreds of students hiding in the building.

"I'm setting up a perimeter by the south entrance. Check in with me there. Lieutenant Ferris has ordered us to wait until bomb squad arrives before entering. SWAT is en route."

John leaned against the building.

I hope the SWAT is Jorgy's team.

The sound of a helicopter approached. John shielded his eyes from the sun as he looked up through the trees.

A news helicopter, circling slowly, trying to get footage.

Vultures.

Mrs. Allison, Tuesday, 11:46 AM

Nancy found the silence eerie. She looked around the classroom and tried to think of something to say. Most of the teenagers were typing into their phones, a few of them were huddled together hugging. Lindsey blew her nose again and threw the tissue under one of the desks.

Nancy watched the Marine as he checked both doors and listened for any sound from the hallway. He walked over to the windows, then sat back down and leaned back against the desk.

Nancy calculated in her head. If he was in Beirut in '83, that made him over fifty. She thought. *Why is it that I never…*

"I joined the Corps in 1981," Clint said, turning to Nancy. "I was just eighteen-years-old. Young, dumb and… well… you know what they say."

Clint pulled out a small box of toothpicks from his front shirt pocket and stuck one between his teeth. He offered one to Nancy.

"No thanks. I'm trying to quit."

"Was shipped to Beirut out of North Carolina in May of '83," Clint said, putting the box of toothpicks back in his shirt pocket, "to continue the, and I quote, 'peacekeeping efforts' between the Shiite Muslims and Israel friendlies. Lebanese Muslims living in Beirut didn't see it that way, especially when four of our Navy warships shelled the hell out of them late September. Muslims were pissed and they wanted payback.

"So the following weeks we were extra careful. Whenever a convoy went out, we were on high alert. But we weren't that worried when we were at our barracks back at the airport. And that's probably what messed us up. We didn't really predict the attack coming to us there. Either that, or we had too much confidence in our chain link fence, our barbwire, and the two sentry posts.

"We had no idea what was coming."

One by one the students looked up from their phones.

"October 22nd – the night before the bombing – I stopped by Willie's food stand to get a Coke. I don't know his real name. He was an old Lebanese guy who ran a concession stand right next to our barracks. He looked dead on a Lebanese version of Willie Nelson. Everyone called him Willie.

"Anyway. Willie was frustrated because a delivery truck backed into his structure as he was closing and now his front bay door wouldn't open. The hinges were bent at the…" Clint waved his hand and shook his head. "Anyway… *the door wouldn't open.* So I told him I'd get my tools and take a peek. Easy stuff. Much easier than the stuff the Corps had me fixing. But it's dark and I was expected at the barracks, so I promised him I'd come back when he opened at zero-six-hundred and fix it before his morning rush. Man's gotta make a livin.'

"I had bought a Coke from Willie every day for five months. He knew I'd be there to help him in the morning. So I said good night to my only Lebanese friend and went inside with my unit.

"The guys were decent spirits that night. Listening to Credence. Whole barracks singing *Have You Ever Seen the Rain,* at the top of their lungs.

"My friend Hambee got a letter from his girlfriend." Clint turned to the teenagers in the room. "This was 1983. There was no Skype or smartphones. The highlight of our week was if someone at home took the time to pull out a pen and a piece of paper and sit down and write us a letter.

"Hambee was going to get married. He…"

Clint's voice faded, and he stared off in the distance for a second.

Nancy looked at the kids in the room. No one was texting or fidgeting. Their eyes were fixed on Clint, the same man they had passed in the hallways probably every day, but never really saw.

Clint blinked twice and cleared his throat. "Well, that's neither here nor there.

"Anyway. The next morning, at five minutes before zero-six-hundred I show up with my tools. I worked on his door for about twenty minutes, but sadly, Willie's hinges were bent so

176

bad they're unfixable. But as luck would have it, I had just fixed a door the week prior at the sentry post—by the front gate—and left the old hinges on the countertop to clean up later. Never did clean it up... *as luck would have it*. So I walk out to the sentry post to see if I can grab em' for old Willie."

"At 6:22, as I'm walking out to the sentry post—the only one in my entire unit *not* in the building. A twenty-ton yellow truck shows up at the airport—one of those old Mercedes Benz stake beds with the little wooden rails around the edge—and starts circling the parking lot. I ask the two sentries about it and they tell me they are expecting a water truck. As it turned out, this truck wasn't a water truck. It was a hijacked truck carrying over 20,000 pounds of explosives.

"Truck begins accelerating and rolls right over the slinky wire and heads for the sentry post. Sentries didn't have time to react. The Rules of Engagement crippled them. The sentries weren't allowed to have a round chambered or magazines inserted, so the truck flew past the post, through the gate and smashes right into the lobby of the barracks.

"Last thing I saw was Willie walking out of his food stand and headed toward me with a Coke bottle in his hand..." Clint paused and got lost in thought for a moment... "and a second later he and the entire building disappeared."

Clint got up and walked over to the window.

"Driver was an Iranian named Ascari. No group every claimed credit for it, but we all knew who did it. Smart bastards. They lined the bed of the truck with marble flooring and rigged the explosives on top of that. When Ascari crashed into the building he detonated it and the marble forced the blast upward. The four-story building collapsed killing 220 Marines, twenty-one other service men... *and one Lebanese*. Me and 127 others were wounded. I was the only one in my unit who made it out alive.

"Less than ten minutes later the French barracks were attacked. Fifty-eight of their paratroopers were killed as well.

"The bombing was the worst single-day death toll for the United States Marines since World War II's Battle of Iwo Jima,"

Clint turned around and looked at the teenagers. "You know…
the famous battle, and the statue of the Marines holding up the
flag?"

"Every kid in this school probably knows about Iwo Jima…
but the 242 who lost their lives in Beirut…"

Clint didn't finish this sentence. He just turned back toward
the window.

Brett, Tuesday, 11:50 AM

Brett checked the next door on his right. It was locked. He backed up to shoot the doorknob but heard a sound from down the hall toward the music room.

He walked into the music room and flicked on the lights. Several kids were crouching behind a set of bleachers. He didn't recognize them. They looked like freshman or sophomores, skinny and a little awkward.

Brett aimed his shotgun toward the trio. "Stand up. Now!"

All three stood up with their hands raised. The one on the right began whimpering.

Brett felt a lump form in his throat.

So much blood already.

As much as he had tried to convince himself that everyone was guilty, he struggled locating the enmity required to pull the trigger on these three.

"I've got an idea," Brett suggested walking into the middle of the room.

He lowered his shotgun and whispered. "I'll give you guys a chance."

He pulled out his Glock. The three winced at the sight of the weapon.

"I'll count to three before I start shooting."

The three kids looked at each other.

"Ready?" Brett said. "One…"

The kids took off sprinting across the music room toward the hallway.

"Two…"

The kids were almost to the door.

"Three!"

Brett emptied half of his magazine as they disappeared around the corner, hitting nothing but sheetrock.

He sighed and cued another song up in his playlist.

Teenagers My Chemical Romance

But if you're troubled and hurt, what you got under your shirt will
make them pay for the things that they did…

Brett exited the music room, turned back toward the hallway
he had just come from and tried a door on his left. It was locked.
He backed up and shot the doorknob with his 12-gauge. The
door swung open.

Brett slowly peeked inside. It looked empty. He quickly
checked the blind corner, then entered the room. It was open
and uncluttered. The teacher's desk provided the only place
where anyone could hide.

The bell rang, scaring Brett. He looked at the clock.
11:53. End of lunch.

Funny how fast time flies.

Brett heard a helicopter in the distance. He walked toward the
windows but caught a glimpse of movement in his peripheral
vision. Brett swung his gun in that direction. Two students were
sitting on the ground behind the desk… one, an old friend.

"Stand up," Brett whispered, disguising his voice, and pointed the shotgun at them.

Nick got up, but Cordell just sat there.

"I said, stand up!" Brett tried again.

"I'll stay seated, thank you," Cordell said calmly. Not looking
at the masked gunman.

Brett didn't know how to respond. No one had stood up to
him yet today. Cordell's lack of fear was unsettling.

"Stand," Brett ordered. Leaning the gun a little closer.

"Don't push it, Brett!" Cordell bellowed, turning toward the
masked gunman.

Brett paused for a second when he heard his name. *How did he
know?* The mask obviously wasn't a foolproof disguise. Brett
knew this. He had considered using a better disguise, but the
mask would be sufficient enough to buy him the few minutes he
needed when the time came.

Brett's hesitation was noticeable.

"Do you think that gun scares me?" Cordell barked. "Ya think I ain't never had a gun up in my face before?"

The masked gunman held his position.

"I'm sorry you're having a bad day," Cordell said. "I'm sorry that these people don't treat you right. But so what! I ain't been treated right my whole life. And you don't see me waving a gauge up in this piece."

Brett took a step back, still holding the gun on Cordell. Brett wasn't expecting this confrontation. The gun was supposed to command respect. *No gun, no respect,* he repeated to himself. *That's why I always got the gun!*

Cordell stood up and faced Brett. "So if you got some business to take care of, then take care of it. And if you gonna shoot me…" Cordell threw his arms in the air. "…then get it over with!"

Brett flinched, but held his position.

"And if you ain't going to shoot me," Cordell continued quietly. "Then get outta my face. Cause you know I ain't ever had a problem with you." Cordell leaned against the wall and folded his arms.

Brett was relieved when Cordell leaned back. It would have been easy to just squeeze the trigger if he needed to. But his own weapon—fear—had just been used against him. Even though Brett was the one with the gun, using it on Cordell was harder than he had predicted.

His gut was twisted in knots. First the three boys, now this confrontation. This wasn't what he expected. His heart felt like it was going to burst from his chest.

Brett adjusted his fingers on the trigger.

Nick stood up and took a careful step forward. "Brett," he offered kindly. "Whatcha doing, man?"

Brett kept his stare at Cordell, but moved the gun to Nick, who froze in his tracks.

"He speaks," Brett declared, using his normal voice. "Funny, I don't think you've spoken to me since junior high. Your timing is… uh…suspicious."

Nick nodded his head back and forth. "Come on, man. You know it ain't like that. I've never done nothing...."

Brett turned his stare toward Nick. "That's right," he snapped loudly. "You've done *nothing*. You've passed me in the hallway hundreds of times, you've watched them tease me, hit me, spit on me..." Brett paused and looked around the room. "...hundreds of times, and you've done absolutely nothing. You've never objected in any way. You've never spoken up. You've never made the slightest effort. It's true, Nick, you've never done nothing. A true bystander."

Nick swallowed hard and took small steps backward. His hand wiped a tear from his cheek.

Brett actually felt something for his old friend. He remembered all the times they used to stay up late playing Halo and stuffing their faces with everything microwavable. The two of them used to hang out all the time. But how times change.

Now Brett controlled Nick's destiny in his fingertips.

What power.

Life or death... *all in the tip of his finger.*

Brett considered killing him just to make a point. No one was innocent. Even bystanders. All were guilty.

But his gut twisted tighter. Nick didn't need to die today. There was a fate worse than death.

Brett lowered the gun. "You never know — this whole thing..." Brett pointed all around him, "...maybe it could have been avoided." Brett leaned in toward Nick. "Remember that when you go try to go to sleep tonight."

Brett left the two of them in silence.

Kari, Tuesday, 11:52 AM

Kari looked at her phone again. Still no service.

"Do you have service?" Kari asked, holding up her phone.

Michael pulled his phone out of his front pocket and checked. "Nothing." He rubbed his head, confused. "How is that even possible?!! I just had service in the student center. That's probably less than a hundred yards from here."

Kari looked around the room, noting the air units. "Do you think it's these machines?"

"Shouldn't be. Maybe it's just these walls." Michael looked at the walls from where he sat. They were brick. No windows, and one steel door.

The bell rang. The two of them looked at each other.

"End of lunch." Michael said, thinking about where he would normally be at this time.

Michael rebooted his phone and waited for any sign of cell service.

Nothing.

"Do you have any signal at all?" Michael asked, holding up his phone. "Even one bar?"

"Nothing." She said, without even looking at her phone.

Michael paused for a moment, debating whether he wanted to get into it with her. "Well, can you at least check?"

Kari sighed, frowned at him, and checked again. "Nothing. Like I said."

"Really? You gonna be like that?"

"Like what?"

Michael just sighed, shook his head, and turned the other way.

Kari scowled. "What's your problem?"

"Honestly? It's that I'm stuck with you, of all people."

"What's that supposed to mean?"

"It means exactly what I said. I'd rather be stuck with anyone else. Literally, anyone!"

"Oh," Kari said, "I'm sure you've got people lining up to be stuck in a closet with you."

"I shoulda just stayed with Sierra and all of them." Michael mumbled, mostly to himself.

Kari paused. "Sierra Blake?"

Michael looked at Kari skeptically. "Yeah."

Kari sneered. "Now, that figures."

Michael leaned forward, obviously heated. "Figures?" Michael scoffed. "Bitch, please!"

"Oh. What a surprise. I'm a bitch now. Is that all you and your thug friends can come up with? We're all bitches?"

Michael stood up. "Thug friends? Is that what you white girls think of us. *We're all thugs?*"

"Don't make this a race thing!" Kari argued.

"I'm not the one using the word *thug*."

"I'm a *bitch*, but you're offended by *thug*?"

Michael paused for a beat. "I'm offended by you dissing on Sierra, acting like you're all that! Do you even know Sierra?"

Kari wavered.

"That's what I thought." Michael snapped. "You walk around this school condescending us, and bitch... you don't even know us!"

"Condescending?" Kari squealed.

"Yeah. Condescending. You want me to define it for you?" Michael mocked.

"I know what it means."

"Because you live it!"

"Where...?"

Michael didn't let her finish her sentence. "Yesterday. Mr. Hunt's class. Something about Brett should take a shower?"

"Seriously?" Kari fired back. "The whole class was laughing. What? You've never said anything bad about anybody?"

Michael snorted. "You're such a hypocrite."

"Hypocrite?" Kari shook her head. "Where did you make that leap?"

"Probably when you were telling the world about your church, and then five minutes later cheating and talking trash."

Kari was dumbstruck.

How did he...

"And don't try to deny that you're a cheater," Michael continued. "I guess your little act of going to church, praying to Jesus, and going on your little trip to help the poor kids is just that — *an act!* Because when it comes down to it, you're just the same as every one of us. You copied those vocabulary answers off Stephanie with no hesitation."

He sat down and crossed his arms. "So think twice before you condescend, Church Girl. We're all on to you!"

Kari turned the other way, trying to avoid sight of him. His words cut deep. She didn't know exactly why... probably because they were true.

He sounded like he was done with his little rant. She hoped he was, because she didn't think she could take one more word.

She felt tears start to stream down her face.

He was turned the other way, so she just let them flow.

She closed her eyes.

This was stupid. All she could think about was how much she would rather be anywhere than in this closet with him. Maybe the hallway wasn't such a bad place right now.

She hated him.

Hate!

Or maybe she just hated what he said.

Michael, Tuesday, 11:55 AM

Michael pretended he didn't notice her, but it was hard to avoid. She didn't say a word, didn't even wipe her tears. She just sat there crying.

Michael clenched his teeth. He tried to fight it, but he couldn't. It's a funny thing — when you yell at someone, even someone who deserves it, you don't feel any better?

The air units stopped.

Silence enveloped the room like a dark cloud. The two of them listened but heard nothing.

Michael crept over and put his ear up to the door to see if he could hear any better.

Nothing.

It seemed like police would be making noise if they were here.

He sat back down quietly, trying to avoid making a sound.

Kari sat looking at her phone. Michael checked his as well. No service.

He watched her scroll through her phone. Her tears stopped flowing, drying on her cheeks. She actually had a really pretty face. Michael had never really been this close. Her eyes were really big, and her lips were... *no matter.* If they belonged to someone else, he might have been interested.

Part of him felt bad for laying into her, but another part argued that she deserved it.

Did she really?

She was basically guilty for doing what everyone else in this school did: cheating and talking about other people.

But Michael had done both the previous week, too.

Maybe I was the hypocrite.

Maybe everyone was a hypocrite, and Kari definitely wasn't the worst, compared to the way Luke, Blake, and Tyler treated...

"Brett!"

Kari, Tuesday, 11:58 AM

The two of them sat in silence on the cold cement floor. It had been minutes since either had talked.

Michael's words hurt. As much as she wanted to hate him for what he said... she knew he was right.

She welcomed the monotonous whirring of the air units. She peered around the room. The big machines, whatever they were, were loud and enveloped most of the small closet. Ductwork crept from the machines to the ceiling. Kari stared at a piece of insulation hanging down from one of the air ducts blowing in the breeze created by one of the fans. It looked like the cotton candy she liked so much at the California State Fair.

Great fried Twinkies. Kristen always likes...

Kari gasped.

Kristen!

Where was her sister? Her sister had B lunch. That meant she was supposed to be in class right now... in this building!

Kari tried to remember what class. She didn't know her sister's exact class schedule.

She pulled out her phone again, hoping for some sign of cell service. No bars.

Her shoulders dropped. She felt completely helpless.

Please be okay.

She closed her eyes and said a prayer for her sister. When she finished, she opened her eyes again, wishing that somehow, she wouldn't be stuck in this closet, but home with her family. She missed Mom, Dad and Jordan.

I actually miss Kristen.

She clicked on her texting icon and began scrolling down through the names. Even though there was no service, she could read old texts. Somehow, they were comforting.

She found a text from Kristen last week.

Kristen: Where are you? I've gotta go.

Kristen sent it from the car after church last Sunday. Kari had been hanging out talking with her friends after church and Kristen was in the car waiting. Kristen didn't care for church, probably wouldn't even go each week if it wasn't required, so she was always first to the car.

Kari scrolled down through the texting trail reading past conversations between her and her sister.

Kristen: Where's my white sweater?

That was the beginning of a huge fight.
She kept scrolling.

Kristen: Wanna grab Panera?

Kari recognized this conversation from a little over a month ago after track practice one afternoon. Kari's dad made Kristen pick her up from track every once in a while, when needed. Kristen was in a rare good mood that day and had a carbohydrate craving. Kari smiled as she read the text trail.

Kari: Yaaassssss! Come get me.

Kristen: If you're gonna eat bad, might as well go big.

Kari: Hahaha. True! I might just get the broccoli cheese bread bowl.

Kristen: Fatty!

Kari: Anorexic!

Kristen: Whore!

Kari chuckled to herself. Kristen might have…
Michael spoke up, interrupting her thought. "Brett!"
"What?" Kari asked.
"You said you didn't see any shooters, right? But people were saying someone was wearing a mask, right?"

"Yeah. So."

"So," Michael said. "If you were to vote who in this school is most likely to go around wearing a mask on a vengeful shooting spree... who would you guess?"

"Oh my gosh. You're right! It's got to be him!"

"Gotta be," Michael said.

"What do you think he wants?"

"Probably to kill Luke, Blake and every other tool bag in this school!"

Kari's face sank. "What about cheerleaders?"

"Since when do you care about cheerleaders?"

"My sister."

"You have a sister?"

"Yeah," Kari said. "Kristen."

"Here?" Michael asked, pointing down. "At this school?"

"She's on Varsity cheer."

Michael looked surprised. "Your sister is a Varsity cheerleader?"

"Why is this so shocking?"

Michael shrugged his shoulders. "I don't know. I guess... you just didn't seem like the cheerleader type."

"I'm not. My sister is."

"I guess I just never pictured you with a cheerleader sister."

"I'll take that as a complement. But yes, sadly I ride to school every day with my sister, Taylor Withers, and..."

"Taylor Withers?" Michael interrupted.

"Yeah. So?"

"What does your sister look like?"

Kari pulled out her phone, scrolled down to a photo of Kristen, and handed the phone to Michael.

"I just saw her," Michael said, pointing to the phone. "Like fifteen minutes ago in Mrs. London's classroom."

"Is she okay?"

"Yeah. She's safe for now. She's with Taylor, Sierra, Ryan, Matt, and a few others. The door's barricaded."

Kari sighed. "Thank God! Wait. How did you get in if their door was barricaded?"

"With the keys through the teacher's lounge."

"Couldn't Brett... or whoever the shooter is... get in through that door also?" Kari asked.

"I don't think so. At least, I didn't see a bunch of doors busted open. Besides. Didn't you hear that explosion? I bet the cops are already here. I haven't heard anything for a while."

Michael walked up and put his ear to the door.

Silence.

Investigator John Grove, Tuesday, 12:10 PM

"How many minutes until bomb squad gets here?"

"Just a few. Ten tops." Lieutenant Ferris confirmed. "Who do you have on crowd control?"

"I've got Parker and Stephens. Parents are starting to show. Are you sending me more units?"

"They'll be there in literally two minutes. And SWAT in three."

"Gotcha."

"Keep me posted, Grove."

"Will do, Lieutenant."

John hung up the phone. He was excited to hear Jorgy's team was on the way.

His phone vibrated.

Manda: How was your big drug bust this morning?

John: Flawless.

John paused. He didn't make it a habit to tell Manda when he was in the middle of something. It only caused worry.

John: You are my sunshine.

Manda: Am I your only sunshine? Do I make you happy when skies are grey?

John smiled.

John: ☺ Gotta go. LUV U.

Manda: I love you more!

John heard movement, someone running up behind him. He pulled his gun and turned.

"Whoa!" the man said, skidding to a stop and raising his hands. "I'm just trying to get into that building."

The man was in his late twenties, Caucasian, good-looking, sharp dresser, with a gold Tag Heuer watch. He was breathing heavy and looked flustered.

"Not now, sir," John said. "I don't know how you got up here, but you need to head back down to the parking lot, now!"

"Please," the man begged. "My wife. She's inside."

Kari, Tuesday, 12:10 PM

"I have to pee."

Michael raised his eyebrows. "How long have you had to pee?"

"Long."

"Well hold it," Michael said.

"I can't."

"Yes, you can."

Kari clenched her teeth and looked at Michael with wide eyes. "I can't!"

"Well what do you want me to do, go out in the hallways and say, 'Time out everyone! Kari's gotta pee!'"

Kari rocked back and forth on her haunches. "I don't know."

"Well, hold it then."

"Michael, I swear, we're both going to be sitting in a puddle if you don't find something for me to pee in."

Michael's eyes grew large. "In here?"

"Got to. I'm going to explode."

"How do you get from zero to 'I'm going to explode' in like five minutes? Where was, 'I kinda gotta pee,' then, 'I really need to pee,' and..."

"Just find me something!"

"Like what"

"Anything!"

Michael got up and looked around the small room. He grabbed a five-gallon bucket off one of the shelves. "This is coated in dry paint, but it might do. It might not be comfortable to sit on, but..."

"I'm not going to sit."

Michael paused. "What do you mean you're not going to sit? Isn't that how girls pee?"

"I'm going to hover."

Michael tilted his head. "Won't that be difficult?" He looked at the bucket and grabbed the edge. "Look, you can sit right here..."

"I'm going to hover. I do it all the time."

"All the time?"

"Yeah." Kari responded, nodding. "All the time."

"Like here at school? You never sit?"

"Nope. Hover."

"Wow. Do you hover everywhere?" Michael asked.

"Pretty much."

"At the mall?"

"Hover."

"Movie theatres?"

"Hover."

"Church?"

"Hover."

"Port-a-potties."

"Definitely hover!" Kari said.

"Where don't you hover?"

"Home."

"That's it?" Michael asked.

"Yep."

"Damn, girl. You must have some strong legs."

Kari grabbed the bucket and got up. Looking around the room, she eventually crawled behind one of the big air units.

"Don't look."

"Why would I wanna watch you pee?"

"'Cause guys are sick bastards. Just don't!"

Michael laughed. "True. But no problem. I ain't looking."

Kari unbuttoned her pants, pulled them down, started to squat, but hesitated. "Cover your ears."

"Why?"

"I don't want you to hear."

"Oh my God."

"Just cover your ears. And stop using the Lord's name in vain."

Michael sighed and covered his ears.

"Are your ears covered?" Kari asked from behind the vent.

"Yes."

"Then how did you hear me ask?"

"Seriously? Just pee! I'll cover my ears!"

Brett, Tuesday, 12:10 PM

Brett walked through the student center. It was vacant now. Music was still playing. The DJ had abandoned her post.

> *Queen & David Bowie*
> Under Pressure

Brett didn't know the song. Sounded like Vanilla Ice. The beat was catchy.

And love dares you to care for the people on the edge of the night, and love dares you to change our way of caring about ourselves. This is our last dance…

He checked behind the couches and in the one blind corner behind the DJ booth. He saw no one. He used the opportunity to load another handful of shells into his gauge to keep it full.

His pocket buzzed.

Interesting. Brett rarely received texts or calls. Who could be texting him?

Brett checked his six, then retrieved the phone from his pocket. It was his mom.

Batshit Crazy: Brett. Are you okay? What's going on?

Brett paused. His mom never texted him. *Ever.* He didn't really know what to think of the text.

Before he had a chance to reply, another text came through.

Batshit Crazy: A policeman was here, and now we just saw on the news that there is a shooting at the school.

Brett thought for a moment, then typed a quick reply.

Brett: Someone is on campus with a gun. I'm hiding in a room at school. I hope he doesn't find me. I'm so scared!

Brett hit SEND, then watched his screen.
Within seconds three dots appeared. She was typing.
Twenty seconds later his phone vibrated again.

Batshit Crazy: Stay hidden! Please don't do anything
stupid. The police are coming!

Brett: Don't worry about me. I'm staying hidden.

Brett tucked his phone away and headed toward the north stairwell. As he rounded the corner, he surprised Blake and Deeby running full sprint toward the student center. When they saw the masked gunman, they stopped dead in their tracks and put their hands up.

"Easy, man. We didn't do nothing," Blake said.

"That's what everyone keeps saying," the gunman said, in a soft disguised whisper.

"Hey man. It's cool. Really..." Deeby begged.

The gunman paused for a moment, hesitating, then turned towards Deeby. "You're a movie expert, right?"

Deeby looked surprised. He glanced at Blake, then back at the masked gunman. "Not really. I mean, maybe. I don't know. Do you want me to be? I mean... name it. I'll be it."

"I'll tell you what," the gunman offered. "If you can answer three movie questions, then you live."

Deeby started shaking. "I don't know, man. I mean..."

"I could just shoot you both right now if..."

"Okay, okay!" Deeby interrupted. "Three questions. Definitely three questions."

Brett walked around the two students, gun raised and keeping a safe distance.

"Question number one. What was the name of the guy in *Full Metal Jacket* who everyone teased until he finally committed suicide?"

Deeby raised his hand.

"You don't have to raise your hand," the gunman said.

"But I have a question," Deeby said.

"What?"

"Do you want the actor's name, the character's name, or the character's nickname?"

The gunman snickered. "I want the character's name—the same guy they all called Gomer Pyle before pelting him with bars of soap when he went to bed."

"Leonard Lawrence!" Deeby said quickly. "His name was Leonard Lawrence, played by Vincent D'Onofrio!"

"Very good. Correct."

"Yes!" Deeby cheered. "Hey! Do I get an extra point for knowing the actor?"

"Nice try. And obviously too easy, so... question number two: What was the name of the actor who played the nerdy kid who got beat up by the bad guys in *The Punisher*?"

Deeby jumped up and down, raising his hand.

The gunman sighed again. Deeby looked at his own hand and quickly retracted it.

"Sorry! No hand. I keep forgetting. He was played by Ben Foster, who was also amazing in *3:10 to Yuma*, by the way. Kind of showed up both Russell Crowe and Christian Bale, don't you think?"

"Damn, you're pretty good at this," the gunman said.

Deeby smiled. "Check out the name tag. You're in my world now, Grandma!"

"Question number three: What was the name of the lonely female lead character in the movie *The Girl with the Dragon Tattoo*?"

"The Swedish version or the American version?" Deeby asked.

"I don't know that..."

"Aaaaaaaaaaaaaaaaagh!" Deeby screamed.

The gunman jumped back, holding the gun on Deeby. "What the hell was that?"

"Sorry. I was just quoting *Monty Python's the Holy Grail*. You see, this guy had to answer three questions to cross the Bridge of Death or he would be thrown into the fire, and when the Bridgekeeper asked King Arthur what..."

"Enough." The gunman interrupted, in a scratchy voice. "Do you know the answer or not?"

"I'm sorry. I'm just so nervous. "Her name is Lisbeth in both films."

"No," the gunman said. "It's Elizabeth."

"No, it's not," Deeby argued. "Look it up. It's Lisbeth. Look it up."

"I don't have to look it up. It's Elizabeth. I've got the gun."

"Wait! Wait! I'm just getting my phone," Deeby cautiously pulled his phone out of his front pocket and began punching some keys.

"I didn't say you could do that."

"Yeah, well I figured I have nothing to lose because it sounds like you're going to kill us anyways." Deeby kept typing into his phone. "Aha. Look here!" He held out his phone to the gunman. "I'm assuming you saw the American version, and you can see that her name is Lisbeth even in that version." He pointed to the phone. "See? Lisbeth. Her name is Lisbeth."

The gunman leaned in, tilted his head and looked at the phone.

Deeby kept talking. "If you would have seen the Swedish version you would have known that because it was subtitled, and her name was on the bottom of the screen every time..."

"Okay... you can go," the gunman said.

Deeby stopped mid-sentence. His eyes lit up. "Seriously?"

"Yes."

The two of them both started to go, but the gunman placed the barrel on Blake's chest, telling him, "Not you, just him."

Deeby disappeared down the hallway and shouted, "Hasta la vista, baby!"

Blake turned back toward the gunman and begged. "What? I can't answer any movie questions."

"I have a different question for you, and it's easy, because you know the answer," the gunman whispered.

"Sure. Anything. What's the question?" Blake asked respectfully.

Brett found the respect entertaining. For years Brett had only heard a belittling tone from Blake, Luke and the rest of them. But now, everything was different. Brett, his mask and his 12-gauge had discovered a newfound respect.

Brett couldn't help himself. He used his normal voice.

"First, I need you to get on your knees."

Blake quickly dropped to his knees, but then his expression changed. Brett could see the recognition on his face.

"Brett?" Blake asked.

Brett calmly opened the shotgun and began loading shells. Blake's face contorted to that of a whimpering child. Tears flooded his eyes. Brett witnessed something he never had seen before in Blake. *Fear.* Absolute Fear.

Brett slowly loaded three more shells into the gun while Blake extended his hand out, a futile defensive maneuver: "Please, man. I'm sorry."

Tears rolled down his cheeks.

Brett cycled the action on the shotgun. Blake flinched at the sound. Brett proudly lifted his mask for just a second so Blake could see his eyes. When Blake saw him, he began shuddering and shut his eyes quickly as if trying to wake up from a nightmare.

"And here's your question."

Brett leaned in close to Blake.

"Where's Luke?"

Blake stopped breathing for a moment. He couldn't breathe and think at the same time. It was too much.

"Where's Luke?" Brett asked again, pressing the shotgun against Blake's head.

Blake began whimpering and shaking. He didn't respond.

Weak. I knew he was weak!

"Where?" Brett demanded. "This is the last time I'm going to ask!"

Blake cowered again like a cocker spaniel that was just caught piddling on the floor. He slowly raised his right arm, pointing down the hallway. "In the bathroom just over there by the north stairwell."

"Thank you," Brett offered softly.

The shotgun blast echoed throughout the hallway.

Investigator John Grove, Tuesday, 12:18 PM

When Jorgy and his men heard the shot, they stopped prepping their gear for a moment.

"Sounds like a 12-gauge." Jorgy offered.

"I've been hearing plenty shots just like it is coming from in there in the last hour." John said.

John and the team finished prep in a matter of seconds. While waiting for the bomb squad, they studied a map of the building and the personnel list the school administration had given them. Names, room numbers, background information… name it. They wanted every piece of information possible about who was in this building. Everything helped.

Two ex-military were in this building – one, a decorated Marine.

One of the ex-soldiers was the wife of the rogue yuppie who John almost shot a few minutes prior when the man broke the perimeter and snuck up on him. John asked the man a few questions about his wife and then had him amiably escorted back to the parking lot by one of the arriving officers.

Bomb squad's head tactical advisor approached John: "I'm Jacob Earnst. Bomb Squad. Where's the device?"

"Let me show you."

John crept up to the wall adjacent to the door and pointed toward the door. "It's attached just inside the door. But watch yourself. The shooter can see these doors for almost 100 yards down that hallway."

John peeked around the corner and motioned the coast was clear.

The tactical advisor slid over to the door and peered down at the device. His eyebrows rose curiously.

Earnst turned toward John. "Watch my six. I'm going to cut the glass for a better look."

John kept his eyes peeled down the hallway watching for any movement. Meanwhile, Earnst cut a perfect circle and peered his head through to get a closer look at the device."

After about 5 seconds Earnst pulled his head from the hole reached in and grabbed one of the two devices. He pulled the wire out, yanked it off the door and tossed it to John.

John flinched, catching it. "What the hell you doing?"

Earnst laughed. "It's a timer hooked to an empty box."

John raised his eyebrows. "It's another decoy?"

"Expensive decoy. Those timers aren't cheap. And that housing is another three digits. Kid's committed."

John turned to Jorgy. "You know what this means?"

Jorgy turned to his men. "Guys, we're going in."

Sierra, Tuesday, 12:18 PM

The room was still. The two cheerleaders were leaning on each other with their eyes closed, and the girl in the red sweater had actually stopped crying and lay down. The haphazard group had probably almost convinced themselves the nightmare was over, and then a single blast echoed from the hallway — the first one in a long time.

The girl in the red sweater sat up, eyes wide. "Do you think that was the good guys?"

Matt shrugged his shoulders. "Or the bad guys."

Sierra's phone began vibrating in her pocket — more than normal. Someone was calling. Sierra pulled out her phone and looked at the screen.

Nicky

She answered quietly. "Hey. You okay?"

"Angelica's dying."

"What? How do you know?"

"I don't." Nicole said. *"But there's blood all over the place, she's acting really crazy and she wants someone to do her last rites."*

"Her last rites?"

"Yeah. That's what she said. No one here is Catholic, so we don't know what to do. She's starting to freak out. Don't you go to church?"

Sierra shifted on her haunches. "Not really. Like Christmas Mass."

"Well, does anyone else there go to church? Someone needs to talk to this girl."

Sierra cupped her hand over the phone. "Um... does anyone here know how to give last rites?"

"That Catholic thing?" Matt asked.

"Yeah."

Everyone in the room just looked at each other.

"What's going on?" The girl in the red sweater asked Sierra.

"Angelica Chavez is dying. She wants someone to do her last rites."

Everyone stared at Sierra. "She's scared, okay. She wants her sins forgiven and shit. Is that so unreasonable?"

Everyone just sat there.

Taylor nudged Kristen. "You go to church every week. Talk to her."

"I'm *not* Catholic," Kristen said. "I'm Presbyterian. We don't do that."

The voice on the phone called for Sierra. *"Sierra? Do you have anyone there or what?"*

Sierra put the phone back up to her mouth. "Sorry, Nicole. We only have a Presbyterian. No Catholics."

"That will work. Put her on."

Sierra looked at the phone, shrugged her shoulders and handed it to Kristen. Kristen took it hesitantly.

"What? I have no idea what to do."

Kristen put the phone to her ear. She heard voices talking in the background. Then she heard a girl's voice come on the line. *"Hello?"*

"Hi," Kristen said, not really knowing what else to say.

"Hi. Who's this?"

"It's Kristen Ridge."

"The cheerleader?"

Kristen looked around at the people in front of her. They were all watching her. "Yeah."

"Oh wow. You're beautiful." The voice said.

Kristen surprised herself with a smile. "Thank you. Who is this?"

"This is Angelica. I had you in Computers last year."

"Oh yeah, I remember you." She mouthed to Taylor: *I have no idea who this is.*

"I need someone to give me my last rites."

"Are you sure?" Kristen asked. "Maybe you're going to be fine."

"Nope. This is it. I can tell. Please give me my last rites."

"Okay," Kristen said, taking a deep breath. "How do you do it?"

"I have no idea."

"Well, then how do you know you need it?"

"*Because in every movie I've watched, when a Catholic dies they get last rites. And my abuela is going to kill me if I die without doing my last rites.*"

"Okay," Kristen said, assuring herself more than Angelica. "We can do this. We're going to pray, and you're going to confess any sins you've committed."

"*That's it?*"

"Yep."

"*Are you sure?*"

"Yep," Kristen was actually telling the truth for the first time in this conversation.

Taylor Withers leaned in close to Kristen and grabbed her arm. "Are you sure that will work? If she really dies and you told her the wrong thing, that's on you!"

"Trust me," Kristen said, covering the phone with her hand. "This worked for the guy who died on the cross next to Jesus — it'll work for Andrea."

"Angelica!" Sierra corrected.

"Whatever."

"*How do I do it?*"

"Just tell God you're sorry and ask him to forgive you."

"*God or Jesus?*" Angelica asked.

"Same guy," Kristen said.

The voice said a small prayer. "*God, I don't know if you know me, but it's me, Angelica. I'm pretty messed up and I need some help. Can you please forgive me for cheating in Mr. Dawson's class, for stealing my cousin's earrings, for talking about Britney behind her back even though she did the same to me, for lying to my mom about my Tinder app, for sleeping with Zack...*"

Kristen held the phone down and mouthed to Taylor: "This girl's worse than me!"

"*...for getting in a fight with my sister, for skipping mass so much, and...*" the phone went silent for a few seconds. "*Oh... and for sleeping with Nick, Jared and Brandon.*"

"Okay," Kristen said. "Now all..."

The voice interrupted her. "*And Chris.*"

The other end of the line was silent. Kristen broke the silence. "Is that it?"

"*I think so.*"

"Why don't you say, 'forgive me for all my sins' just to be sure?"

"*Oh, cool. That's smart. 'Forgive me for all my sins.' Now what?*"

"Just say 'Amen!'"

"*Amen.*"

"All done!"

Kristen hung up, handed the phone back to Sierra without even looking at her, and began brushing some lint off her cheer uniform.

Michael, Tuesday, 12:18 PM

A gun blast shook the hallways.

Kari covered her ears with her hands. "I thought maybe this was over."

"Me too," Michael said. "It's been a long time since the last gun shots. I was hoping he... *they*... *whoever*...was gone."

Kari looked at the door. "That one sounded a little closer." She looked worried.

Michael stood up and pressed his ear against the door again. He couldn't hear a sound.

"These boxes are heavy," he assured her, pushing on them. "And this door is solid. No one's getting in this room. You chose wisely." He sat down and leaned back against the wall.

Kari's gaze looked at the boxes, as if she was inspecting everyone. Then she looked at Michael. "You chose wisely, too."

"Dumb luck," he told her honestly. "I just happened to be in front of the door, and Large Marge just happened to have dropped..."

"I'm sorry," Kari interrupted.

"For what? Peeing in front of me?"

"I didn't pee in front of you," Kari insisted.

"You were like five feet from me."

"I wasn't *in front* of you."

"I don't know," he smiled. "That stream was pretty loud..."

"I thought you had your ears covered!"

"I did. But it didn't do any good. It was like trying to cover your ears at Niagara Falls."

Kari hit Michael in the arm, with a hint of a smile on her face. The two laughed.

She stared down at her shoes. She was wearing white Chucks. She rubbed one toe on top of the other.

"I'm trying to apologize for earlier."

Michael looked over at her. She just kept staring at her shoes.

"You were right." She said, finally looking up at Michael. "I..."

The fans kicked on, with a loud screech. Kari jumped up and almost fell backward. Michael put his hand on her shoulder to stop her fall. She put her hand on her chest and exhaled in relief.

"Those stupid things scared the poop out of me."

Michael chuckled. "*Poop?*"

"Yeah. I've said worse." She said.

"Oh really. When?"

She sat back down. "I don't know. Like the time my sister put her foot through the bathroom door trying to break in."

"I knew she was vicious."

"Really?" Kari asked skeptically. "I'm not disagreeing with you, I'm just curious how you came to that conclusion."

"I know things about people."

Kari laughed. "So what do you know about my sister?"

"I don't want to go talking about your sister."

"No. The door is already open on this one. Tell me what you know."

"Well, she's friends with Taylor Withers, for one," Michael said. "And that girl's a ho!"

Kari feigned like she objected but couldn't hide a smile.

"She's had more boyfriends than Taylor Swift!" Michael added.

"Yeah, but at least Taylor Withers doesn't write songs about her exes."

Michael laughed. "True. But still a ho."

"And she's a cheerleader," Michael continued. "And cheerleaders, by definition must lack some moral fiber."

"Oh really?" Kari said, smiling. Michael was pretty sure she actually agreed with him but wasn't willing to admit it. "Probably true. Not Megan, though."

"Megan Parks?"

"Yeah. Do you know her?"

"Yeah. Well, kind of," Michael said, scratching his head.

"How?"

"My cousin, Bobby."

Kari tilted her head. "Bobby? Bobby who? Does he go here?"

"Did last year. Bobby Lotomau? He was in a wheelchair?"

"Oh. *That* Bobby," She said, surprised. "He's your cousin?"
She hesitated. "I mean... isn't he... Mexican?"
    Michael shook his head. "You white people are hilarious."
    "What?"
    "Anyone who ain't black or white are Mexican to you."
    "That's not true," Kari objected.
    "Okay," Michael said. "Then name someone of another race!"
    "Sue Kim." She said quickly.
    The two of them paused and looked at each other... then
burst out laughing, covering their own mouths so
they wouldn't be too loud. Although it didn't matter. Michael
could have played a drum solo in that room and no one would
have heard him over those fans.
    "What kind of test was that?" Kari said, still laughing.
    "I have no idea. But you passed." Michael said, still chuckling.
"But no, Bobby is not Mexican or Korean for that matter, he is
half Samoan."
    Kari looked confused. "Then how is he your cousin?"
    "My mom's sister? She met this Samoan guy in Oakland...
anyway. You get the idea."
    "So how did we get on Bobby?" she asked.
    "Megan," Michael reminded her. "You asked me if I knew
Megan."
    "Oh yeah. So how is Megan..."
    "She's just one of the only people at this school who was ever
nice to Bobby," Michael said. "And not just once. *Always* nice."
    Kari nodded her head. "That sounds like Megan."
    "I remember one time Bobby was in the cafeteria and he need-
ed help getting his tray. I was over with Cordell and the fellas..." Michael wavered, telling this part, "and in all honesty, I
just didn't feel like getting up and helping him.
    "You know how Bobby was, always asking people to help
him get his food and carry his tray for him, and you know how
irritated people got. I mean, not at first. Everybody would help
the wheelchair kid once. Maybe even twice. But let's be real. If you
were in line and you saw

Bobby coming, you'd be like everyone else… *and suddenly have to go to the bathroom.* Because if you volunteered to help Bobby, you had to stand in line with him, get him his drink, find him a place to sit… *helping Bobby was a commitment!*

"Well, no one was in line that day, and no one was about to get up and help him, including his cousin…" Michael said, pointing to himself.

As Michael told her this story, he remembered the instance clearly. He remembered exactly what he was thinking that day, he remembered the expression on Bobby's face…

People are bastards.

Michael shook his head.

"But then Megan sees him." Michael continued. "She gets up from her table of cheerleaders. She walks over to Bobby and she offers to help. And Bobby…" Michael laughed, just thinking about it. "He's taking forever. 'Can you get me a scoop of this?' and 'No potatoes.' and 'Do you have whole milk? Well, then can you get some from the back?'"

Kari laughed at Michael's Bobby voice. He was pretty good at it.

"And Megan is standing there with him the whole time. And you know what she did when she was done helping him?" Michael asked.

Kari shook her head.

"She *sat* with him!" Michael said, leaning forward. "Have you ever sat with Bobby for a meal?"

"No," Kari said, smiling. "What?"

"He's boring as hell!"

Kari laughed. "That's so mean!"

"How's that mean? I've eaten more meals with the kid than anyone in the school. He's a boring-ass brutha! It's not because he's handicapped. If he was a player in the NFL I still wouldn't want to eat lunch with him. Conversation with Bobby is so dull it's painful!"

Kari laughed some more.

Michael sighed. "And you know what?"

"No. What?"

"I've seen Megan eat with him like a dozen times. By herself. When she had a whole table of friends she could have sat with.

"Megan is..." Michael searched for the words to describe her.

"Pretty?" Kari said, popping her eyebrows.

"What's with the eyebrows?" Michael asked. "I mean, I know she's pretty. Stevie Wonder knows she's pretty. But don't ever do that eyebrow shit again."

Kari laughed again. "You're funny."

Michael smiled. "I know."

She laughed even harder. "No, I mean it. You are really funny. I can't believe I've never talked with you."

"You were scared of talking with a black guy. Admit it. You thought I was going to steal your purse."

She hit his arm playfully again. "That's so unfair!" She paused. "I thought you were going to carjack us, actually."

"Oh!" Michael laughed, covering his mouth. "She made a funny!"

The two of them sighed then sat in silence for a moment, taking it all in.

It was weird. It was one of the most frightening days of their lives, but something unexpected was happening... the two of them were somehow finding comfort within the barricade of brick, tile, and steel.

"She goes to my church," Kari said, breaking the silence.

"Who, Megan?"

"Yep."

"Really?" Michael couldn't picture that. He didn't know why, but he always pictured church people as... *different*. Except maybe for Nana.

"Yeah. She's even going to Mexico with me next week."

"Well, you should put Megan on your church poster, because then more people would go."

"Because she's so pretty?"

"Nope. Because she's Megan. She cares about..." Michael searched for the right words.

"The least of my brethren." Kari said. "The words you were looking for. Jesus said, 'whatever you do to the least of my brethren, you do unto me."

Michael pondered her words. "Jesus said that?"

"Yep."

"That's good. So, yeah. Megan cares about the least of the brethren. And if your church was full of Megan's, I'd go. I'd even bring my boring-ass cousin."

"Would you take him to lunch afterward?" Kari said, smiling.

"Hell no!"

Investigator John Grove, Tuesday, 12:24 PM

Jorgy finished briefing his men. He gave the signal and his lead man reached through the glass hole and quietly opened the door.

John checked his weapon. He had never followed Jorgy's team twice in one day before.

As the team disappeared into the building, John followed.

A thunderous shotgun blast echoed from upstairs.

Jorgy stopped his team and gave a few hand signals.

The team split. One third hung a left and headed for the south stairwell, and the rest continued down the hallway.

Two more gun blasts echoed from upstairs.

The team on the stairway looked at each other, then continued up the stairs. By the time they hit the top of the stairs they heard a fourth blast. It sounded like it was coming from the far north end of the hallway, out of sight from the team.

The downstairs team stepped over the three bodies just inside the lobby. John stopped and checked pulses. All three were long gone.

The plan was to make a sweep of the hallways first and neutralize the shooter. If for some reason the shooter wasn't found, they'd start clearing rooms one by one and evacuating into a holding area.

The first door on the right was open. The team leader peeked in, checking the corners first. Then his gaze stopped. John couldn't see what the leader was looking at, but he could tell it was upsetting.

"My God," he said. Then he gave a signal to keep moving.

As the team members passed they each peeked in the door. Their eyes each grew in size as they peered in. The second to last officer almost tripped as he gazed a little too long.

John passed the door and gave a quick glance.

Bodies. Probably 20 in one classroom.

Far too many young bodies.

John hadn't seen anything that awful since Kuwait, something he had spent over a dozen years trying to delete from his flash memory.

And with a hand signal, the team continued down the hall.

Michael, Tuesday, 12:24 PM

Michael's stomach gurgled. Kari must have heard it because she looked up at him. The two of them laughed again.

Michael's gaze fell on her. She really had beautiful lips.

"I guess my Cocoa Puffs weren't enough this morning," Michael finally said, attempting to thwart any chance of awkwardness.

Her eyes got big. "Cocoa Puffs? No way. Me too."

"Really?" Michael couldn't picture her eating Cocoa Puffs. She seemed like a bagel and cream cheese girl or some something like that.

"Really," she said, wiping her nose with one sleeve, and then doing her famous eye dabbing motion with her other sleeve. He had seen her do it multiple times. "I scarf Cocoa Puffs."

"That's funny. What? They don't have Snow Puffs or something like that for white girls?"

She smiled. "No, I tried Snow Puffs. They were pretty bland. I prefer Cocoa Puffs."

This girl was full of surprises.

"What does your mom ... or your mom and dad do?" Michael asked.

Kari sat up straight and stretched her arms. "My mom is a stay at home mom, and my dad works at HP. What about your parents?"

"My dad developed a software company," Michael said with a straight face. "He makes millions. We're set for life."

"That sounds like an okay job," Kari responded, clueless of his sarcasm.

Michael shook his head. "He's on welfare, Kari. He's never shown up for anything. Nothing! He's a real piece of shit."

Kari blinked twice. Her mouth opened a little, but she didn't say anything.

Michael let her off the hook. "Don't worry 'bout it, Kari. My mom's always taken care of us. She works at a bank. She works hard. Always provided for me and Tish."

"Tish?"

"My sister, Tisha." When Michael said those words, Kari's stare drifted toward the door. Her thoughts were elsewhere.

"What?" Michael asked.

"Kristen." She whispered.

Kari started biting her fingernails; she was in deep thought. Michael felt bad for her. He understood. He'd be worried if Tisha were somewhere in these hallways.

He tried to change the subject.

"My mom got robbed once."

"Huh?"

"My mom. I told you she works in a bank? She got robbed once."

She stopped biting her nails for a second. "What happened?"

"Most robbers are stupid. They go in and hand a note. Crazy, but almost all robbers use notes. That way they don't have to use their voice. No ski mask, no visible gun, just a note. And almost every note has three common words on it. Guess which words."

Kari just stared at Michael.

"Guess!" he prodded her.

"Oh," she said, off guard. "I thought you were being rhetorical."

"Guess," He insisted.

"Okay, okay. Ummm…" she puckered her lips and scrunched her face, in a concentration pose.

Suddenly Michael found himself entranced by her. She had the most perfect little baby face you'd ever seen. Pretty like her sister, but more innocent. Her sister was hot, but like 'stripper' hot. Not the kind of girl you wanted to bring home to mom. Kari, however was beautiful, and Michael was pretty sure she'd continue to grow even more so.

"I don't know," she finally said, rolling her eyes, trying to guess. "Give me money!"

Michael chuckled. "Money. That's one of them."

"I give up. What are the other two words?"

Michael leaned back. "*Money, gun,* and *the f-word.* FBI found that almost every robbery note has those three words in common. They all want *money*—there's word number one. And they all have to show force. If you tell a bank teller across a big ol' counter that you have a knife, the teller will be like, 'So what? You gonna jump over this counter and stab me for my money?' So the robber always says he has a *gun*—there's word number two. But the robber also has to show everyone that he's serious. That's why they use the F-word. If your note just says, *Can I please have your money, I have a gun!* that ain't scary. But if your note says, *I have a gun. I want you to put all your money in the bag. If you make a sound, I'll blow your effing skull off your neck!* Then people listen.

"Mom's only been robbed once. It was a white dude with a scraggly beard."

"Sorry about that." Kari interrupted.

"Sorry about what?"

"Sorry that a white guy robbed you," she smiled subtly. "All of us white people know each other. We're part of this under-ground organization..."

"The KKK?" Michael jibed.

Kari pointed at Michael. "That's not funny." Then she smiled again.

Michael continued where he left off. "So this white, bearded, hick, redneck, pasty, country music-loving..."

"Okay, okay!" she said. "I get the point!"

"...walks in and handed her a note. Mom says she had a bad feeling about the guy. He wore his sunglasses the whole time in line and she had never seen him before. Everyone knew every-one at her small branch. But Momma helped him, and sure enough... *a note*. And guess what three words the note had in it?"

Michael paused and waited for her to answer.

"Money, gun, and the F-word?" Kari answered. She listened like a good student.

"Excellent. You have a future in law enforcement."

Kari nodded her head. "I always had my heart set on being a mall cop."

Damn, she was cute.

Michael smiled and continued. "Momma gave him the top drawer. Idiot didn't even know to ask her for the bottom drawer. That's where all the big cash is."

"Why don't the robbers just steal from the main vault?"

"Good question. Because that takes guts. It's simple to walk in with a note and three words. But to actually pull out a gun and force someone to open up a vault ... that almost never happens.

"But check this out. She says that on some Mondays she will count $30,000 or $40,000 in deposits in the first hour because..."

Michael and Kari were interrupted by the sound of an ear-piercing blast. It was so loud Michael's ears rang for what seemed like a minute. Kari reflexively put her hands over her ears. She started to say something, but Michael put his finger to his lips, motioning for her to be quiet. The fans were still going, so their small movements weren't...

Raised voices.

Screams.

Two more shots... really close. They almost sounded like they were coming from the walls or the ductwork in the closet, not outside the door.

Kari started breathing really heavy. Michael scooted over to her and put his arm around her, and she buried her face in his chest.

Less than a minute later another deafening blast shook the walls.

Kari sobbed into his chest and her whole body started shaking. Her heart was beating so fast, it was exploding from her chest. Michael could feel it against his body.

The doorknob wiggled.

The two of them froze.

She stared into Michael's eyes. He brought his finger to her lips and mouthed, "Not a sound." Her eyes looked terrified. She didn't need to say a thing; her face said it all.

The door was locked, and apparently that was good enough for the person on the other side because it stopped moving and they didn't hear another sound.

Seconds turned to minutes. They didn't move a muscle. Michael and Kari just sat there staring at each other. It was probably the most scared Michael had ever felt in his entire life, but for some reason... *there was no place he would have rather been.*

Joel Cruz, Tuesday, 12:27 PM

Freshman Joel Cruz debated whether to finally come out of the supply cabinet. It had been several minutes now since the shots and he hadn't heard a thing.

Joel was using the bathroom when the first shots echoed through the hallways. He heard screams and people talking about someone shooting students, so he quickly looked for a place to hide. The cabinet in the corner of the wall had plenty of room, so he slid some cleaning supplies over and crawled in, unnoticed by anyone.

It wasn't long before he heard a group come into the bathroom and begin arguing about the safest place to hide. Some stayed and some left. He didn't recognize the voices, so he stayed silent the whole time. They didn't sound like the types who would welcome him. What if they told him he couldn't hide in there?

Two of the guys talked a lot, the third didn't say much other than, *"Shut up!"* Then all three would argue about whether or not their talking would draw attention to the shooter. In the middle of one of these arguments a deafening blast blew open the door and then a new voice entered the room. There was arguing, screaming and then two more earsplitting blasts.

Two voices remained. One pleaded while the other laughed. One more blast.

And now silence.

Joel thought he heard the door shut after the shots, so the shooter probably had left.

But what if he hadn't?

Could the shooter still be in there waiting?

Joel couldn't feel his left leg anymore. He tried to move it and accidentally kicked something by his foot, which tipped over, clanking forcefully.

He froze.

Nothing.

Surely somebody would have heard that.

Joel decided it was worth a peek.

He pushed the cabinet door ever so slightly. Light cascaded from the gap. His eyes adjusted. Something was there leaning against the cabinet.

Joel froze once again. Was this the shooter sitting, waiting for him?

Joel looked cautiously. The body was sitting completely still and had blood tricking down the neck. Joel waited without moving.

Minutes passed.

Nothing.

Joel pushed on the cabinet slightly, and the door pushed on the body's shoulder. The body began tilting away and eventually collapsed flat on the floor. Joel pushed the cabinet door wider until finally he was able to look around most of the room.

Three bodies lay on the floor. Two were upper classmen he recognized and the other was wearing some sort of torn mask and had a gun in his hands. Another gun lay on the ground next to him. Blood seeped out of the mask and pooled onto the tile floor.

Joel slowly stepped out of the cabinets and tried to stand. It was hard because his left leg was completely asleep.

His eyes stopped on the bodies of the two upperclassmen. He didn't know their names, but they were athletes. One of them had put Joel's friend Marcus in the garbage can outside the music room. Both were clearly dead. One body was contorted in a position Houdini would envy.

But Joel couldn't see the third guy's face. From the looks of the gun in his hands, he had committed suicide.

Joel had never seen a dead body before, or three dead bodies, for that matter. He began to feel woozy. The air was stuffy.

Need fresh air.

Joel sprinted for the door, opened it, and took one step into the hallway... only to be staring down the barrel of a small, black, automatic weapon.

Deputy Williams, Tuesday, 12:27 PM

Deputy Jared T. Williams moved through the hall silently, leading his team cautiously toward the north stairwell.

Jared had been a cop for twelve years, on SWAT for three. He had seen his share of death, but nothing like this.

He reflected on his own children, eight and ten. They were at their school right now, not four miles from Mesa.

What kind of monster would do this?

He readjusted the grip on his weapon, noting he was gripping it a little tight, maybe a little too much emotion.

His team followed close behind.

As he approached a bathroom door, he heard a noise. He put a fist up, signaling his team to stop. Everyone froze.

Footsteps from inside the door.

The door opened, and a small Hispanic teen burst out of the room... then skidded to a stop, staring at Deputy Williams' MP-5.

"Hands in the air."

The student's lip quivered, and he backed up against the wall.

Two of Williams' men turned the student around and frisked him.

"What can you tell us?"

The men kept the questions generic. They had no idea who was standing in front of them, although they were pretty sure they were looking at a victim, not a perp.

The kid just whimpered, crying audibly now.

Deputy Williams walked up to the boy and talked like a dad, not a cop. "What did you see, son?"

The boy didn't say a word. He just pointed to the bathroom door.

"Is there anyone alive in that room, son?"

The boy closed his eyes tight, trying to make it all go away. He shook his head no.

Williams commanded one man to stay with the boy, then he turned to the door. He opened it cautiously, gun first, and entered using standard protocol.

He kicked the 12-gauge out of the one teen's hands, sliding it to the back corner of the room, and did the same with the AR-15. No other weapons were visible. When the room was secure he checked the pulse of the three bodies. All were dead.

He walked to the corner of the room and placed the back of his knuckles on the barrel of the shotgun.

Warm.

The AR-15, cold.

He spoke into his lavaliere mic.

"Papa Bear, this is Goldylocks. I've possibly got the perp's body here. I have the two weapons matching the description. Possible suicide. White male, maybe six-feet tall, athletic, wearing an alien mask... and wrestling shoes."

Investigator John Grove, Tuesday, 12:29 PM

"…white male, maybe six-feet tall, athletic, wearing an alien mask… and wrestling shoes."

Six-foot? Athletic? Wrestling shoes?

John had never met Brett, but that didn't sound like a description of him.

John grabbed his radio. "Goldylocks, this is the Woodcutter. Can you give me a hair color for the perp in the alien mask?"

Ten seconds passed.

The radio squawked. "Woodcutter, this is Goldylocks. Copy that. Let me check. Give me two shakes."

Silence.

Lieutenant Ferris' voice came through the radio. "We've got some injuries downstairs that are a priority. I'm sending EMT's through the East Entrance with SWAT in the cleared south classrooms."

Sadly, this wasn't the radio chatter John needed.

Squawk. "Papa Bear, this is Little Red, I've got more bodies, North stairwell."

Squawk. "Copy that Little Red."

Silence.

Squawk. "Papa Bear, this is Baby Bear. I've got a young man here hiding in the girl's bathroom who had a face to face with the shooter. I'm bringing him to you."

"Squawk. "Hey… *Red Leader, this is Gold Leader*… give me that… *Sorry, I just have always wanted to…*"

The radio squawked again and then was silent.

John tapped his foot impatiently.

Come on… come on.

Austin Walters, Tuesday, 12:36 PM

Austin and Trevor began hearing more voices now — adult voices.

"That's gotta be good, right?" Trevor whispered. "It's probably help!"

"I think so. Let's check it out."

The two freshmen slid out from behind the large countertop in the back of the art room. The small classroom was overstuffed with supply cabinets and easels, a result of combining classrooms, thanks to California State budget cuts. But the boys weren't complaining, the cluster offered plenty of places to hide.

They heard a police radio in the distance. The two looked at each other and smiled.

As they walked toward the door a cabinet creaked open to their left. A sandy blonde head poked out of the cabinet and panicked when he saw the two boys.

"Please! Don't hurt me! Don't hurt me!"

Austin shook his head. "Chill, man. We were hiding, too."

"I think it's safe now," Trevor added.

"But how do we know they aren't still out there?" the blonde kid asked.

"Because we just heard the police in the hallway," Austin said. "Come on."

The blonde kid crawled out of the cabinet. "I can't believe we're safe."

"I know," Trevor said. "We hid when we first heard the shots. Never even closed the door. We heard everything!"

"A couple times we think we even heard the killers walk in here and look around."

"Our spot was pretty good though." The two boys gave each other a high five.

"Man, we're so lucky!" The blonde kid added. And gave them each a high five.

The three of them walked out into the hallway.

"Hold it!" a voice shouted from the hallway. The three boys put their hands up.

Mrs. Allison, Tuesday, 12:36 PM

Nancy almost jumped when she heard the knock at the door. Clint leapt up and quickly pressed up against the wall next to the door. He quietly reached for the sharpened wood dowel he had strategically set in the corner by the door, holding it with two hands, ready to strike at anyone entering.

"Sacramento sheriffs!"

All the kids looked at Nancy with hopeful eyes.

"What's the code word?" Nancy asked through the door.

Clint looked at her skeptically and mouthed, *code word?*

"Yeah," Nancy whispered. "I forgot about it until now. We had an in-service last year. They're supposed to use a code word if..."

"Boiler room."

Nancy tilted her head. "And there it is."

"Did anyone ever notice that the 'code word' is actually two words?" Clint asked.

She stood up and walked to the door. "Before I slide all this out of the way, do you mind telling me who you are so I feel a little more at ease?"

"Will do, Sgt. Allison. I'm Officer Brady of Sacramento County SWAT. I just talked with a Derek outside who's very eager to see you. And I must say, we were very happy to find out there was a soldier on campus."

Nancy choked up, tears of joy. "Thank you, officer. *Two* soldiers."

"It's an honor. I'm glad to hear you're both okay," he said. "You can open this door when you're ready. We will be here for you. But use caution. We still don't have confirmation on the shooter's location."

Clint looked at Nancy. She looked at her .380. "Maybe I should keep this handy."

"I've got an idea," Clint said.

A minute later Nancy cautiously opened the door to discover two SWAT officers waiting in the hallway.

"Ma'am, I am supposed to escort you all out of the building and we need to keep you all accounted for and in the debrief area once we are outside. Understand?"

"Yes," Nancy said.

"Have you had these students in your sight the entire time?" the officer asked.

"Yes."

"Okay. And are you the only adult with them?"

"Yes," Nancy said.

"Okay, please come with me."

Investigator John Grove, Tuesday, 12:38 PM

John watched EMTs rush into a downstairs room near the south stairwell. Other classrooms were being evacuated one at a time and taken to a holding area.

What was taking Goldylocks so long?

John headed down the hall and up the north stairwell to take a peek for himself. As he stepped onto the second floor, his radio squawked.

"Woodcutter, this is Goldylocks. Peeked under the mask. Brown hair. Has a wallet. California Driver's License says Luke McCormick. Can't tell if it's a match…" The voice on the radio hesitated. "No face to match it too, sir. But the two weapons are lying next to him, and the mask matches the description we've heard from more than a dozen students."

"Copy that, Goldylocks. But I don't think that's our shooter."

John cursed and pulled the radio away from his face.

Where's Brett?

He looked down the hallway. SWAT was starting to escort students from various classrooms. Lines of students were marching toward the two stairways.

Several groups of young students, possibly freshman or sophomores, were walking single file toward the south stairway past John. They all looked atypical for teenagers. Quiet. Orderly. Following directions.

"Head right for that stairway," The SWAT officer instructed the line of students. "Just keep straight."

John looked in every student's eyes and found one common denominator: *terror*. These kids had been to hell and back. John had been there, and he recognized the facial expression.

Every kid… *except for one.*

He recognized those eyes. Small dark eyes darting right and left, pushed down by a heavy brow.

It's him!

John called, "Brett!"

Brett, Tuesday, 12:39 PM

Brett couldn't help but notice how good it felt to breathe without a mask on.

He and his two new friends walked with their hands on their heads as commanded, but he was careful not to lift his arms too high, exposing the Glock he had shoved in the back of his pants. *Stupid cops never even frisked them.*

More students were escorted into the hallway. They all were being ushered outside. His plan was working perfectly.

A plainclothes cop was standing in the hallway watching. Brett didn't do anything to stand out. He just followed the kid in front of him. But the cop was staring right at him.

Something's wrong. This guy knows something.

A group of EMTs rushed past the line of students. Then another three SWAT members. One stopped and talked with the officer who was leading Brett.

"Head right for that stairway. Just keep straight," the officer commanded, then turned to talk to one of the passing SWAT guys.

The black officer kept staring at Brett.

Brett contemplated drawing his gun, but there were about half a dozen cops with guns in the hallway. Not a good place to go all *Kill Bill.*

Then the black officer looked right at him and said, "Brett!"

He knows!

Another classroom of kids walked in between the cop and Brett. Brett took the opportunity and slid out of rank, leaning out of sight up against the wall and reaching for his gun.

As the last student passed, Brett lifted his gun at the black cop. He had a direct shot, and the cop must have realized it, because his eyes grew large.

Investigator John Grove, Tuesday, 12:39 PM

Brett's eyes gave him away.

When Brett heard his name, his face told the rest of the story.

John couldn't figure how Brett had managed to blend in with the rest of the students unnoticed. Where had he come from?

No matter. The rampage was over. Brett was trapped now, surrounded by cops. John knew far more about Brett's exploits that day than Brett even fathomed.

John would take him quietly.

Another line of students walked past, blocking John's view for a second.

John blinked.

Brett was gone.

John's heart stopped. How did he...

John turned.

And there was Brett standing up against the wall, gun drawn. Brett had him, dead to rights.

Brett just stared at John, with a hint of a smile.

But Brett's smile was premature. A red dot glided up Brett's neck and landed on his cheekbone.

"Not quite, son," a voice said calmly from John's left. "Put your weapon down."

John turned to see a man in a white T-shirt, holding a gun with Brett in his sights. The man had a Marine Corps tattoo on his right bicep.

Brett's eyes darted back and forth, but he kept his gun on John.

"It looks like we have ourselves a Mexican standoff." Brett said.

"Actually, that's not true." John said. "In a Mexican standoff I would have a gun too. Would you like me to draw mine, so we can do this right?"

"You're pretty funny for 5.0." Brett said. "But sorry. You just keep your hands where I can see them. In fact, our janitor friend here..."

"Corporal Clint Havard, United States Marine Corps."

Brett shot a quick glance at the Marine, then readjusted his hands on his gun.

"I..."

Brett's sentence was stopped short as the door to his right opened.

Michael, Tuesday, 12:37

For the first time Michael and Kari began hearing voices outside of the doors. It was difficult to decipher with the sound of the fans, but when Michael pressed his ear against the jam, he thought he heard adult and teen voices.

"What do you hear?" Kari asked.

"Voices. Lots of them."

"That's got to be good, right?"

"I think so. I mean let's think about this," Michael reasoned. "There is no way we'd be hearing a bunch of calm voices if there was a shooter still roaming around, right?"

Kari thought about his words and nodded her head. "Yeah, right."

Without saying another word, they both started moving boxes away from the door.

With just two boxes left, Michael's phone rang.

"You have got to be kidding." He gasped. "Now? It works now?!! Unbelievable!" He stopped and looked at his screen. It was his mom.

He answered it. "Mom?"

"Michael? Is that you?" It was his mom's voice. She sounded really stressed.

"Yes, Mom. It's me. I'm fine."

"Oh, thank God! I'm watching the news right now and I've tried you like a million times. Tish and I are going insane!"

Michael felt bad, but Kari was lifting the last two heavy boxes by herself.

"We're fine Mom. We've been hiding, but we hear voices outside now. We're going to check it out!"

"No, Michael! Stay where you are!"

"Why?"

Kari moved the last box and headed toward the door.

"They haven't found the shooters yet. It's written across the screen right now. They're still searching for them."

Kari mouthed to Michael, *I'm going to find Kristen.*

Michael held his hand up to stop her, whispering, "Wait, my mom says it's not safe yet."

Kari waited.

"Mom, are you sure? The stupid news doesn't know. We can hear voices in the hallway right now. I think it's safe."

"*Don't chance it, Michael...*"

Kari was starting to look antsy. She whispered. "Michael, I've got to check on my sister. I'll be fine."

Michael held up his hand signaling her to wait.

She sighed and rolled her eyes.

Michael gave her the international *please* look with his eyes.

She sighed again and put her hand on her hip, then mouthed. *Hurry up.*

"Mom, I'm going to be..."

"*Just a second, here's Tish.*" Michael heard his mom pass the phone to my sister. "*Michael! Don't trust nobody. Mr. Sanders was just interviewed. They haven't found anyone yet and they're literally trying to find him right now...*"

Kari waved to get my attention, whispering, "I'm going."

Michael held the phone aside for a second. "Kari. Don't. My sister says they haven't caught him and..."

"Michael, I'm just going a couple doors down to Mrs. London's room to get Kristen. I'll come right back, okay?"

"No! Just..." Michael heard his sister yelling in the phone. He tried to give Kari the *wait-one-second* sign with his finger, but she leaned forward and kissed him. Not a long kiss, but not just a short peck, either.

The perfect kiss.

"I'll be right back Michael. I promise."

And she turned the doorknob, disappeared out the door, and closed the door behind her.

And just like that... *she was gone.*

Brett, Tuesday, 12:40 PM

The door immediately to his right opened.

The timing couldn't have been any more serendipitous. Kari, a girl from several of his classes, stepped out backwards, oblivious, shutting the door carefully. She stepped right into the janitor's line of sight.

Brett saw his opportunity and took it.

Kari, Tuesday, 12:40 PM

"I'll be right back Michael. I promise."

Kari unlocked the door and slipped into the hallway closing the door quietly.

She didn't even see who grabbed her, she just felt an arm wrap around her neck and pull her backward.

The next few seconds were even more confusing. The janitor had his gun pointed at Kari, and another man began yelling, a black man dressed sort of like a teacher, but with a badge hanging on a chain.

The individual who grabbed her pulled her against his body. He slammed back against the door and slid into a corner where the door met a column sticking out of the wall. A gun pressed against her temple and his breath quickened against the back of her neck.

The plain-clothes cop had his gun drawn now, too, and pointed at what Kari thought was the right side of her face.

Please don't shoot.

She closed her eyes.

A familiar voice spoke firmly from behind Kari. "Put the gun down or Kari meets God!"

Brett.

Michael was right.

His arm tightened around Kari's neck, almost choking her. The gun pressed even harder against her temple. She winced.

"Ow!"

Kari heard people running toward her. She opened her eyes.

The cop raised his hand in the air as numerous SWAT officers ran up behind him, their guns aimed toward Kari as well.

Why does everybody have to be pointing their guns at me!

Brett was pressing himself perfectly in the corner with Kari blanketed in front of him. His face pressed so hard against her, she felt his lips move on the back right side of her head.

"Drop the guns now or we get to see what Kari's brains look like."

The plain-clothes cop spoke again. "I can't do that Brett. Let's just talk about this."

Kari winced as Brett screamed, "No more talk. Drop the gun or I . . ."

"Brett!" the cop interrupted. He hesitated for a second and blinked several times. "I brought your dog! Your mom said you'd want her with you."

The room went silent. The only sound Kari heard was heavy breathing in her ear. Then Brett spoke in disbelief. "You what?"

The cop cracked half a smile. "I brought Molly ..."

Investigator John Grove, Tuesday, 12:41

"I brought your dog! Your mom said you'd want her with you."

John was lying through his teeth. He didn't even know why he said it. But he was desperate to connect with this kid... and it seemed to be working.

Brett was silent for a moment, as if he had left his body and went somewhere else. He blinked and wiped his forehead on the girl's shoulder, then looked at John with a confused look on his face. "You what?"

John's mind raced about what to say next. He hoped conversation about his dog—the one thing he might actually value in this life—might distract him from his current state of mind. Who was he fooling?

I have no idea what I'm doing.

John gave it another shot. "I brought Molly. She was in your room when I stopped by your house. I saw her dog bed at the foot of your bed. You obviously take good care of her."

Brett didn't seem convinced. He just stared back at John with that chilling, furrowed brow.

"She's lucky to have you." John said.

"Thanks Dr. Phil. But that doesn't change anything." Brett said.

So much for the dog approach.

"You want the truth?" John asked. "I'll give you the truth. I think the reason you have a dog in your room is because you don't have any other friends. I think your best friend is a dog because you can't get any humans to like you! How's that?"

Brett's teeth clenched. He yelled through the terrified girl's hair. "You think that was my choice? Do you think one day I walked to school and said, 'Hey, I think it would be fun to have no friends.' Do you think that's what I did?"

The boy's eyes scanned back and forth. He knew he was trapped.

"Brett," John said, "I know you're..."

"You don't know shit!" Brett screamed. "Do you think it was my choice to stay home at every dance, to miss every party?

Newsflash—I don't get asked to hang out after the game. As a matter of fact—I can't even go to the game. If I do, people throw shit at me. I'm guessing you don't know what that's like Mr. linebacker. I'm guessing that you never had to sit there and pretend you don't care when pizza and nachos hit you in the back of the head!"

Brett wiped his cheeks on the girl's back. Tears flowed from his eyes.

"You probably think that I'm making this up. In 5th grade two kids in my class kept harassing me. I actually was stupid enough to tell my teacher, and she said she would handle it. She gave them warnings. Now I was a rat. Within a week the whole class was harassing me.

"Couldn't play basketball because I wasn't good enough. Couldn't play kickball because they said I sucked! Couldn't even walk around and mind my own business because then they would say, 'Why do you just walk around by yourself all the time? Don't you have any friends?' I was stuck!"

Brett wiped his nose on his sleeve. "In 6th grade Eric Perkins had it out for me. He started a 'Kill Brett Club.' This guy Eric and his little buddy Tim made T-shirts. I kid you not! They drew a picture of my head on the front of the T-shirt and put a gun scope on it. Then they put the initials KBC. Teachers didn't have a clue. But every kid knew. I would hear whispers in the hallways. 'KBC. KBC.'"

Brett paused. The sound of his breathing was louder. His right eye stared at John through the hair of the frightened girl.

"You have no idea how much that hurts? Do you? It sucks!

"When I told my mom they made T-shirts, she actually said, 'No they didn't, honey.'" Tears streamed down his face. "Can you believe that? 'No, they didn't honey.' She didn't believe me. She just said I was going through a rough phase and it would pass soon."

Brett's face turned completely red, and then he yelled. "Well, it didn't!

"In 7th grade a guy named Luke took notice of me in gym class. Ever been hung by your underwear over the shower han dles? Ever been laughed at by everyone in the entire class, including the teacher, who laughed for a solid minute before he asked someone to take me down?

"Well, Luke won't be hanging anyone else by his underwear anymore!" Brett laughed. "And people aren't gonna condescend me anymore. Including this girl!"

The girl began sobbing. "I'm sorry, Brett. I'm so, so sorry!"

Tears continued to flow down Brett's face. Looking at the girl, he clenched his jaw. "I don't believe you."

Brett raised his elbow and pressed the gun against the girl's temple.

John screamed! "Brett—don't do something you'll regret!"

Brett laughed, wiping the tears from his cheeks again with the girls back. "Uh, you're about an hour late!"

Brett, Tuesday, 12:43 PM

The cop attempted to convince Brett of the impossible. "It's not too late, Brett. Just…" But Brett had heard enough.

Brett screamed. "Enough!" and shot into the ceiling! Kari shrieked.

Brett thought it through. *Kari, then black cop, then maybe a SWAT officer or two. Maybe even the creepy janitor.* Brett realized that the SWAT team would probably waste him before he got any more rounds off, but at least he'd get Kari and the cop. At least he wouldn't have to end it with his own gun. Someone else had to finish it, and he would go out in glory of battle, a battle against the callous society that had created him.

Brett leaned back, putting all his weight on the door, trying to keep Kari between him and the numerous guns opposing him. Brett heard a click and suddenly the door opened inward, leaving him tumbling backward into the closet.

The next few moments felt like they happened in slow motion. Brett knew he was falling backward. *Where?* He didn't know. He just had the overwhelming sense that this was the end.

He saw the eyes of the cops surrounding him, the tense, yet weary expressions on their faces, and the sweat dripping from their temples. The hallway that he had walked by practically unnoticed for almost two years now was slowly disappearing from sight.

He felt his body falling back for what seemed like minutes. Yet, he knew that if he didn't bring his human shield with him, he'd be a sitting duck. That's why he had gripped onto Kari's shirt and pulled her back, too.

Halfway down Brett tried to catch a glimpse of where he was falling. He saw a garbage can. Vents. Some sort of maintenance room he had never seen before. He figured there were plenty of rooms he hadn't been in. Today was the first day he had seen a teacher's lounge. Today was the first day he had seen fear in Luke's eyes. Today was the first for many things.

Finally clearing the threshold, he realized the room wasn't vacant. A kid from the basketball team, and a few of his classes—Michael was his name—was lunging toward him. As Brett hit the ground, Kari fell to his side and Brett veered his gun hand toward Michael.

A shot fired.

Michael landed on top of him.

Time stopped.

Breathing. Heavy breathing.

Brett opened his eyes. Michael was still on top of him wheezing. The basketball player lifted his head trying to speak. He managed two words.

"I'm sorry."

As Brett looked into Michael's eyes, he realized the two of them had never talked.

Until now.

"For what?"

Brett barely got the words out and Michael collapsed to Brett's left.

Brett blinked twice.

The black cop and two SWAT units appeared in the doorway.

Brett was now exposed, clinging onto his Glock. Brett saw at least eight little red dots on his torso. That's why he hesitated, then raised his Glock toward the black cop.

Shots.

Pain.

It was happening. This was part of the plan. One of many plans.

Brett had wanted to escape at first to prove that he could do what no other had done. And he had come so close.

How did this cop catch him anyway?

It didn't make sense. Brett wondered what he had missed?

And why was Michael sorry? Michael had never done anything to Brett.

He had never done anything.

More pain.

Almost dizzying.

Death was inevitable. That was something he knew going into this. He was ready for it. At least, that's what he kept telling himself.

Look upon death with favor!

Who said that? Was it… He couldn't remember.

But it was Hunt… no, Mizner who said, "Those who welcome death have only tried it from the ears up." A quotation Brett had mocked. A philosophy Brett had dismissed as false.

But now death had arrived. Unwelcomed.

Mizner was right.

Everything began to look blurry. It was time. But Brett had changed his mind.

I was wrong . . . I don't want to die.

Kari, Tuesday, 12:44 PM

Kari couldn't see anything; her eyes were closed, and her ears were ringing. She hoped maybe she would wake up from this awful nightmare. But as the ringing faded she heard the sound of Michael's raspy breathing and she realized the horror of what happened.

Somehow the door had opened and both Brett and Kari both fell back into the closet. From there... everything was a blur. The echo of the multiple gun blasts was deafening. She never realized how loud a gun was... especially that close.

She opened her eyes and saw Michael lying next to her, eyes open wide. His breathing started to slow down.

"No! Michael!" Kari pleaded, sitting up and grabbing his hand. A tear fell from her cheek and landed on his face.

He blinked. Then smiled.

Brett's body was lying completely still. Blood soaked the front of his shirt. He didn't even get a shot off... *other than the one that hit Michael.*

The black cop started yelling for EMTs in the hallway.

Michael struggled to talk. "I'm sorry," he whispered. His breathing became very slow.

Kari started to talk, but he interrupted, "Tell..."

His face relaxed. He exhaled and was silent.

He can't die, Kari told herself. *Where were those EMTs?*

The fans stopped.

The room was completely silent.

The reality of what happened began to sink in. Was Michael gone? She had only really known him for that day — and she had never felt closer to anyone in her entire life.

Kari buried her face in his chest for the second time that day and wept aloud.

Michael, Tuesday, 12:42 PM

"Tish... I gotta go. It's..."

Tish wasn't having none of it. *"Michael, just shut up and listen to me, please, for once in your life!"* She was crying. He could hear it in her voice. So he let her talk. *"I went to that school. I know Mr. Sanders. He wouldn't go on and say they haven't found the shooter if they had found the shooter. It was a live interview, Michael. That means that someone is still walking those hallways ready to kill. So if you're hiding, just keep hidden! Please!"*

Michael was usually the logical one in the family, but this time, he couldn't argue with Tish. Her words made complete sense. The halls probably were more dangerous than this room.

What Tish didn't realize was her shrewd arguments had convinced Michael he needed to do the exact opposite of what she was demanding.

If Tish was right, then Kari was now in danger. He couldn't just sit in here while she was out there.

Damn, I told that white girl not to go out there. Why don't she listen!

"Tish, I gotta go. I've gotta help someone."

It was kind of funny—his notion to want to go help. He had no idea what he would actually do. He just knew he had to do something. He had spent his whole life being a bystander.

"No!" Tisha yelled. *"Don't help no one. Don't be stupid. Just stay put and wait for help. No one needs your help. Mom and I need your help. We need you to help us by staying alive. So please. Just stay hidden and wait until this guy is caught. Please?"*

Michael didn't know what to say.

"Promise me, Michael."

The fans in the closet shifted cycles and a gust of air blew across Michael's face.

Promise.

Michael felt a bizarre sense of déjà vu. He recalled his quick chat with Cordell's grandmother the morning before. Michael had already made one promise this week.

He thought about Tish's words, and he couldn't help but notice that everything had flipped upside-down. His whole life he had been guilty of looking out for one person — *me*. Every decision he ever made was based on, *'What do I feel like doing?'* And now that he actually wanted to do something completely *selfless*, his family was basically telling him, *"Michael, be selfish."*

And so, standing just inside the door of a maintenance closet, Michael had an ethical dilemma. He asked himself, what was right: Sit on his ass? Or help Kari find her sister and get off this campus safely?

Selfish or *selfless*.

Tisha was crying in the phone.

"Tish?"

She sniffled. *"Michael."*

"Tell Mom I love her and I'm going to be fine…"

"No, no, no, Michael!" Tisha pleaded.

"Tisha!" Michael laughed. "There are hundreds of kids at this school. Stop worrying about just one. I've gotta help someone."

"Michael…"

"Tisha!" he interrupted her, and she actually listened.

"If you see Cordell's Nana before I do, tell her I'm going to make good on the promise I made her for this coming Sunday, okay?"

Tisha didn't say anything.

"Tish?"

He pulled the phone away from his ear.

No signal.

He couldn't believe it. Not again!

He heard movement on the other side of the door.

He held the phone aside, pressed his face against the door and listened.

Raised voices.

It was impossible to hear anything with these stupid fans going.

He put his hand on the doorknob. It was crystal clear. He knew what he had to do. For the same reason he respected

Megan. For the same reason he respected Kari for going out that door. He couldn't just sit here.

Reflecting, he couldn't believe he got on Kari's case. Look at me! *When my cousin needed help, I didn't help.* When Luke, Blake and all those guys were slapping around Brett countless times, *I didn't do a thing…*

That was probably the most sobering thought.

If Michael was correct, and it was Brett out there doing all of this, then Michael knew… *part of this whole horrific event is on me!* Michael could have done something about this numerous times and he never did.

I could have.

I could have… what did Kari call that?

Whatever you do to the least of my brothers…

A shot rang out, just outside the door. Michael jumped back, almost tripping over one of the boxes.

A scream.

Kari!

Michael opened the door.

Investigator John Grove, Tuesday, 1:26 PM

John watched the EMTs rush another student into an ambulance. Gunshot wound. Critical.

He overheard the principle: a 15-year-old African American boy. Basketball player. Honors student. Barely alive.

John shook his head.

Could all of this have been avoided?

He wanted someone to blame.

"Detective Grove?"

John turned. It was one of Jorgy's guys, an officer named Brady.

"You told me to introduce you to the other soldier."

Brady turned and pointed toward the teacher standing next to him, a petite young lady in her twenties. She was standing next to Corporal Havard.

John extended his hand to Nancy. "Sgt. Allison?"

She shook his hand. "Nancy. Please."

"John Grove."

Detective Grove turned to Clint. "And Corporal Havard, I have to thank you again. I owe you my life. I don't know what I would have done if you hadn't come along."

The rugged Marine shook John's hand.

"I hear that you also saved Mrs. Allison and a classroom full of students," John said. "I guess they got it right when they pinned the Congressional Medal of Honor on you. It's truly an honor to meet you."

John saluted Clint.

Clint stood at attention and returned the salute to his fellow Marine.

For a moment, teachers, policeman and members of the press paused, gazing at the meek janitor with fresh eyes.

The moment passed.

"Congressional Medal of Honor?" Nancy asked, turning to Clint.

Clint just looked down at his feet.

"That's right Sgt. Allison," John said. "When the explosion collapsed the four-story building killing 241 servicemen, Corporal Havard worked for the next 36 hours straight with a piece of shrapnel in his leg pulling survivors out of the rubble, even enduring some sniper attacks while they worked. He and the team pulled out over 100, if I'm not mistaken."

"One-hundred-twenty-eight wounded, sir." Clint said, "242 killed."

"Oh. I'm sorry. I read 241," John said.

"It was 241 Americans. But I lost 242 friends that day."

"How many were killed here today, sir?" a teacher standing nearby asked.

"Thirty-seven, plus the shooter," Brady responded.

"That's thirty-eight. A total of thirty-eight students lost their lives today," John clarified.

"Funny how everybody always wants to leave somebody out of the count, isn't it Detective?" Corporal Havard said, putting a toothpick in his mouth.

PART V

"If we love our brothers and sisters who are believers, it proves that we have passed from death to life. But a person who has no love is still dead."

-The Bible, 1 John 3:14

Michael, Thursday, 10:12 AM

Michael woke to the sound of a door shutting quietly and a steady beeping.

He tried opening his eyes, but the glare of the lights forced them closed.

His head pounded.

He reached up to rub his eyes, and when he lifted his arm, he felt excruciating pain in his ribcage.

He winced.

A voice.

"Michael. Move slowly. You've had multiple surgeries."

He knew that voice.

He tried opening his eyes once again, squinting and turning away from the light from his left.

She reached out with a damp cloth and dabbed at his eyes gently. When she finished, he opened them. She slowly came into focus.

She was wearing a plain white t-shirt and her blonde hair was pulled up and knotted on top of her head. *A messy bun,* he thought. I think that's what they call it anyway.

She smiled.

"Where's your Starbucks?" Michael asked.

Kari laughed an infectious laugh. "See. You almost died and you're already cracking jokes."

Michael started to chuckle, but it hurt like nothing he'd ever felt. He cringed, trying carefully not to move any part of his body.

Moving hurt.

He glanced around the room using only his eyes. It was a small hospital room. The two of them were alone... *again.*

"Where's..."

"Your mom and sister were here for like thirty-six hours straight. The doctor finally sent them home at like three a.m. last night to try to get some sleep. The doctor promised them he'd call them as soon as you woke."

"Are they..."

250

She finished his sentence again. "Thrilled that you're alive? Yes! You were shot once. It hit your left lung and broke a rib, but everyone tells us that this doctor is really amazing. You're at Mercy San Juan's trauma center. Doc says you're going to be fine. Breathing is just going to be hard for a while. And sit-ups. No sit-ups."

He laughed again, forgetting his injury, and it felt like a knife in his side.

"See, who's funny now?" Michael managed to say.

"I'm sorry." She reached out and put her hand gently on his arm. "I forgot that laughing hurt."

"Yeah right. It's your evil plan."

She smiled and looked at him with those blue eyes — eyes he had only known for one day. Not even. Kari had the most beautiful long eyelashes.

Kari. It was weird for Michael to even be thinking about her name. He never had really thought about her name in the last few years of passing her in the hallways. Don't know if he had even said it out loud before that day.

What day was it?

Michael looked at her face. Her skin looked soft.

She began stroking his arm with her fingers, as if on cue. He watched her. *She is breathtaking.*

It didn't really make sense. How long were they actually in that closet together? Hours? Minutes?

She looked over her shoulder at the door. "Do you think I should get the doctor and tell him you're awake?"

"Hold up." he said. He didn't know why, but he wanted a few more minutes with her.

"How long have you been here?" he asked.

"Not long. I left last night when the doctor sent us all home…"

"Us?"

"Oh, yeah. Everyone's here. I mean… this whole ward is filled with injured students."

"How many…"

"Died? Over forty now. A couple more died yesterday. Did you know Jessica Claney? A freshman? Or Joe Allbaugh?"

"He was on my basketball team."

She didn't say anything. Her face said it all.

"So... Brett shot all those people?"

She nodded. "Like sixty students. About twenty of them made it. You included."

The air kicked on in the room, not a loud sound, but a sound they knew all too well. They just looked at each other in silence, taking it all in.

It was weird to fathom.

Michael broke the silence. "You know, for a second, when I woke up, I thought it was all a dream. But then I saw your face and knew."

"I know what you mean. I barely slept last night. And when I did, I had trouble deciphering dream from reality." A tear appeared in the corner of her eye and slowly rolled down her cheek.

It hurt, but he reached up to wipe it away.

She smiled.

"This might sound crazy," he said, "but when I saw you, and realized that I wasn't dreaming... I was actually glad. Because it's different now. I wouldn't want it to be the way it was." He didn't know if this made any sense. "I'm sorry if I'm sounding stupid. I..."

"No," she said, shaking her head. "I know exactly what you're saying. I wouldn't ever wish it on anybody, but it happened, and it made me rethink some things in a way I probably wouldn't have if it..." She searched for words. "You know?"

He nodded, then started to think about his friends.

"Cordell?" he asked quickly, suddenly panic-stricken.

She smiled. "He's fine."

"Oh, thank God."

"Literally." She added.

I realized she probably had people she was worried about, like her sister.

"And your sister?"

"Fine."

"Megan?"

"She was shot, but nothing serious. Just her arm. They made her stay, so some other doc can look at the muscle. It's tore up good. She's next door. I just saw her while you were snoozing this morning."

"I'm glad she's okay." he replied. And his mind started to wander.

Megan. *He shot Megan!* Who was off limits, if not Megan? How angry did you have to be?

Was there any excuse for this kind of massacre?

What detonated this kind of hate?

She set her head softly on his good side and stroked his arm gently with her fingers. Her touch was comforting.

The air shut off and the room went quiet. He rested in the rhythm between the steady beeping tones behind him and the soothing sound of Kari's breathing on his chest.

"I'm glad you're okay," he whispered.

"Only because of you," she whispered back.

The corner of his mouth revealed the faint hint of a smile as he drifted off to sleep.

THE END

About Jonathan

Jonathan McKee is the author of over twenty books including *The Bullying Breakthrough* and *The Guy's Guide to Four Battles Every Young Man Must Face.* Jonathan speaks to parents, leaders, and young people worldwide while writing about parenting and youth culture and providing free resources for families on **TheSource4Parents.com**. Jonathan, his wife, Lori, and his three grown kids live in California.

Speaking:
Jonathan not only trains leaders and teaches parenting workshops, he speaks to young people across the world about faith, friendships, social media and bullying. Jonathan even teaches workshops to families like his popular workshop, *"Four Conversations: The Who, What, When & Why of Wise Posting in an Insecure World."* In this 90-minute workshops Jonathan helps parents, teens & tweens in the same room engage in conversation about:
- The friends you're friending
- The pics you're posting
- The screen time you're absorbing
- The affirmation you're seeking

Jump on **www.TheSource4Parents.com** now for more information about bringing Jonathan to your city.

Social Media:
Connect with Jonathan on the following social media sites:
Facebook.com/InJonathansHead
Instagram.com/InJonathansHead
Twitter.com/InJonathansHead

A discussion guide is available for youth groups and parents of teens who want to talk through the major themes in this book from **www.TheSource4Parents.com**.

Jonathan's Previous Book Titles

Books for Students
The Teen's Guide to Social Media and Mobile Devices
The Zombie Apocalypse Survival Guide for Teenagers
Sex Matters
The Guy's Guide to God, Girls… and the Phone in Your Pocket

Books for Parents
The Bullying Breakthrough
Parenting in a Screen Culture
If I Had a Parenting Do Over
52 Ways to Connect with Your Smartphone Obsessed Kid
More Than Just the Talk
Get Your Teenager Talking

Books for Youth Workers
4 Views on Talking with Teenagers about Sex
Ministry by Teenagers
10-Minute Talks
More 10-Minute Talks
Real Conversations
Connect
Getting Students to Show Up
Do They Run When They See You Coming?

Books for the Business World
Can I Have Your Attention?
The New Breed